"How *can* I *not remember my own daughter?*"

Jill bit her tongue, thinking Aiden didn't have a whole lot of memories to draw from in the first place. He'd spent so little time with Maddy.

"How can I not remember you? I don't know where you came from or how we met, when our anniversary is or even what toppings you like on your pizza." He looked directly at her, right into her eyes—a new habit she found most disconcerting. "I'll tell you something strange, though. When I'm with you, I have the memory of love."

Dear Reader,

A special delivery! We are proud to announce the arrival of another story in our year-long bouncing baby series! Every month we bring you your very own bundle of joy—a cute and delightful romance by one of your favorite authors. This series is all about the true labor of love—parenthood and how to survive it! Because, as our heroes and heroines are about to discover, two's company and three (or four...or five) is a family!

This month it's the turn of Shannon Waverly with *Found: One Father*. Next month's arrival will be (#3481) *Baby in the Boardroom* by Rosemary Gibson.

Happy reading!

The Editors

BABY BOOM

Because two's company and three
(or four...or five) is a family!

Found: One Father

Shannon Waverly

Harlequin Books

TORONTO • NEW YORK • LONDON
AMSTERDAM • PARIS • SYDNEY • HAMBURG
STOCKHOLM • ATHENS • TOKYO • MILAN
MADRID • WARSAW • BUDAPEST • AUCKLAND

ISBN 0-373-03475-X

FOUND: ONE FATHER

First North American Publication 1997.

This edition published by arrangement with Harlequin Books S.A.

Printed in U.S.A.

CHAPTER ONE

THEY left the house in a sham of normalcy for the sake of the baby-sitter, but once in the car, their forced smiles crumbled, and they sank into the emotional exhaustion that was the legacy of the worst night of their lives.

At least it was the worst of Jill's. She wasn't so sure about her husband's. She glanced at Aiden from the corner of her eye, resenting his hard, inscrutable profile. Resenting *him* for pushing them to this point.

"Do you mind if I turn on the radio?" he asked, crisply polite.

"No. Please do."

Aiden flicked the radio knob and something symphonic filled the tight space of his sports car, the impractical two-seater he'd bought when she was pregnant—on purpose, she was sure.

If she'd had a choice, they would've been taking her station wagon, especially since she intended to do some grocery shopping after dropping Aiden off at the airport. But her wagon was in the garage today having its brakes relined.

They drove out of their newly developed, lakefront community onto the quiet two-lane road that would take them to the municipal airport on the outskirts of Wellington, the upscale Boston suburb where they'd lived since getting married three years earlier. To the east, bright morning sunlight flickered through the still leafless April woods.

"We don't have much time to wrap this up, Jill," Aiden said in his deep, well-modulated voice.

Turning from the side window, Jill almost laughed.

Wrap up? He sounded as if he was bringing a business meeting to a close.

"What's to wrap up?"

"Lawyers, for one thing. I'd appreciate it if you'd hold off calling one until I get back."

For a moment Jill's heart lifted with irrational hope—irrational, because *she* was the one who'd initiated yesterday's confrontation. But then Aiden said, "We can go see Mark Hillman together. He's always handled our affairs in the past. No need to go to a stranger now."

"Oh." She sighed. "You want us to see a lawyer together?"

"Yes." Aiden pushed his hand through his thick black hair, still slightly damp from his shower. "No sense in our hiring separate lawyers and turning this into a shark fight."

Jill swallowed. Her throat felt raw from crying. "You're probably right. I don't foresee anything either of us would contest, anyway." She paused, and even to herself she sounded mean-spirited when she added, "I trust you won't be fighting for custody of Maddy."

A muscle jumped along Aiden's jaw, yet he managed to reply simply and with his composure unruffled. "No. What about the house?"

"It's yours. You chose it. You made all the mortgage payments. I don't expect to stay there." Jill didn't even *want* to stay there. Not that she didn't like the house. She did. But in the past year and a half she'd spent far too much time there alone and unhappy. It had taken on a bad feeling for her.

"I don't see myself staying there, either," Aiden said. "I hardly need ten rooms. So if you want to stay..."

"No. I'll begin packing immediately."

"That won't be necessary. I'll move out. As soon as I get back. I'm more mobile than you and the baby."

Jill wasn't fooled. Someone else might mistake

Aiden's offer as a gesture of thoughtfulness. She saw it for what it was, his eagerness to move out.

"Take your time relocating," he said. "Stay until the house sells, if you like." He paused, the slightest frown wrinkling his brow. "Where will you go?"

"I'm not sure. Probably back home to Ohio."

Aiden nodded. "I figured." Something in the sureness of his statement made her glance at him. It was almost as if he'd *always* figured she'd be returning to Ohio.

"Where will *you* go?" she asked.

"Probably back to Shawmut Gardens." He was referring to the apartment building where he'd lived before they were married. "I liked the flat I had there." His voice was dispassionate, his expression detached. Jill felt as if she were talking to an automaton. If he was upset by their impending separation, he hid it well—as he hid everything that was important and personal. Even last evening, when she'd been an emotional wreck, he'd hardly argued, hardly gotten upset. The truth of the matter was, he probably didn't care enough to get upset.

Aiden down-shifted the powerful sports car and turned in at the airport gate. As the car made the turn, the sun swept across the windshield and over his face, gilding his features with morning gold. For one unguarded moment Jill's traitorous heart beat in double time.

At thirty-one, Aiden was an uncommonly handsome man, with a masculinely beautiful face yoked to an athletically graceful body, the sort of man who, quite literally, made women turn and stare. In the morning, when he was freshly shaved, crisply dressed and ready to take on the world, he was devastating.

He was wearing his charcoal-gray Pierre Cardin suit today, immaculate and commanding, with a pale gray shirt whose collar was still open and waiting for a tie. The subtle fragrance of a designer aftershave scented the air.

Jill's gaze roamed his features: his dark, perpetually

knit brows; his penetrating blue eyes framed by thick, black lashes; his straight nose; sensuously drawn mouth with its full lower lip; his strong jaw; the chin marked by a shallow cleft.

It was a handsome face—but it wasn't the sum of its features that made Aiden Morse so very attractive. It was something deeper, something insubstantial, a quality Jill could only describe as his presence. She'd felt it the first time she'd met him—his focused drive, his intelligence, his inner strength—and nothing in her experience since had diminished the feeling.

With a start, Jill broke out of her bemusement. Good Lord, what was she doing, sitting here pondering Aiden's virtues? Angered by her lingering vulnerability to a man she no longer loved, she returned her gaze to the road and her thoughts to the business at hand. "The only claim I will make is on Maddy's behalf."

"Child support. Of course. That goes without saying." Aiden guided the sports car into the short-term parking area. "And what about you?" he asked, bringing the vehicle to a neat stop.

"Me?"

"Hmm. You know, alimony."

Jill took in a shivery breath. "No, I don't want anything for myself. I have my college degree and some work experience. I can get a job." Her already bleary eyes burned. She'd always envisioned a busy life for herself, one that someday included getting back out into the workforce. But not yet. Oh, not yet. These first few years of Maddy's life were too precious.

Aiden hung his wrist over the steering wheel and stared out the windshield. "We're probably jumping the gun here, discussing money. That's a lawyer's job."

"You're probably right."

"Sure. Don't worry about that now. Mark'll work out the details. We'll go see him when I get back."

"Okay." Jill glanced at the clock on the dash. Time was slipping fast, yet neither of them moved.

Wearing a thoughtful frown, Aiden said, "I'm going to ask a dumb question, Jill, but I feel it should be asked. Are you sure this is what you want?"

Jill clutched her hands in her lap and thought of the comfort in retreat, the safety in saying no. As painful as their marriage had become, within it she still had security. Going it alone, socially and financially, was a terrifying prospect.

But then Jill remembered the pain, the loneliness, the humiliation of the past nineteen months, the heartache that showed no signs of changing with time. Above all, she remembered Maddy. For her daughter she could do anything.

She lifted her chin and said, "Yes. I see no alternative." She stared at the dashboard, clenching her hands tighter as memories assailed her. "Life isn't supposed to be lived this way, Aiden. You're barely ever home, and when you are, you pay so little attention to us that I feel we're just a pit stop in your schedule."

"Can we do this without resuming the mudslinging?" His voice took on an edge. "I'm well acquainted with your gripes, Jill."

"*My* gripes? You make it sound as if our problems are all *my* doing."

Aiden's mouth tightened to a hard, thin line.

Jill lowered her eyes. "Sorry. I don't want to argue, either." They'd gone beyond arguing.

A few long seconds of uneasiness passed. Aiden finally said, "Who would've thought missing a child's birthday would lead to this?" He spoke with a bitter laugh.

Jill didn't share his twisted amusement. "It wasn't just any child, Aiden. And it wasn't just any birthday. It was her first. Furthermore, don't try to reduce our problems to one incident. Missing her birthday was just the tip of the iceberg, and you know it.'' Her voice was beginning to tremble with anger again, despite her intention to remain calm.

Aiden gripped the wheel in two hands, elbows locked, back straining the seat, and blew out a tight breath. His gaze remained fixed straight ahead, on the terminal across the roadway.

Jill was used to his not looking at her when they spoke. It was just one more sign that he'd lost interest in her. She knew she'd changed since having the baby. She was five pounds heavier, for one thing, tired much of the time, and unable to entertain as she used to. Her style of dress had changed, as well, her silk blouses and heels put away in favor of jeans and sneakers. Nor was there time anymore to fuss with her hair, which was blond and shoulder-length, and which she often tied back or simply left hanging loose. Compared with the polished businesswomen Aiden brushed shoulders with every day, she'd undoubtedly become totally unexciting now that she was ''just'' a housewife and mother.

Still, she didn't look *that* bad. In fact, just recently she'd noticed two teenagers at the supermarket admiring her.

No, the truth was, Aiden just didn't love her, and she seriously wondered if he ever had. He was too careful a person to let emotion rule him. She believed he'd simply reached a time in his life when he thought he should be married—that it might enhance his career to appear settled—and she'd fit the image of what he was looking for in a wife. That, not love, was why he'd married her.

''Just out of curiosity,'' Aiden said, turning so that his back rested against the door, ''mind if I ask a question?''

Jill glowered. ''What?''

''Do you have someone else?''

Her breath exploded in a soft, incredulous laugh. ''Yeah. We've been meeting during Maddy's nap time, between loads of laundry.'' She rested her elbow on the window ledge and dropped her pounding head to her palm.

"You're the one who insists on doing the laundry, Jill. The cleaning woman could just as easily..."

"I'm not complaining about laundry." She closed her eyes. "It's just, that accusation is so..." She couldn't find a word that fit her frustration.

"Well, you can't blame me for asking, the way that *friend* of yours, Eric Lindstrom, has been hanging around lately."

She lifted her head from her hand. "Eric *is* a friend, and I refuse to stoop to a defense of him."

"Fine." Aiden raised his hands in wry surrender. "A young divorced guy just happens to be sprawled on my living room couch every time I come home—who am I to expect an explanation?"

"Aiden, stop it. Eric has nothing to do with this." Nothing, she thought, except that she was able to talk to Eric, laugh with him and share the joy of parenthood. She couldn't remember the last time she and Aiden had done anything even close to that.

Unexpectedly, a wave of sadness overtook her. "I didn't mean to start sniping, Aiden. I don't want us to part like this."

"No, neither do I." Aiden checked his watch. "Listen, I've still got to buy my ticket. Can we continue this inside?"

Jill gave a scant nod and opened her door. Her legs quivered when she got out.

Aiden unfolded his long limbs and got out, too, his six-foot-one frame dwarfing the small car. He reached into the storage area behind the seat, retrieved his garment bag and hooked it over his shoulder. Then he lifted out his briefcase and shut the door.

The air was fresh and fragrant with spring smells—sweet daffodils, new grass, moist, burgeoning woods. On the perimeter of the small airport, the trees were just beginning to bud, the woods forming a haze of palest green. Usually Jill adored spring, but on this particular morning, it seemed a mockery.

They fell into step and headed toward the terminal, she in her casual jogging outfit, Aiden in his expensive suit with the jacket unbuttoned and flapping in the cool breeze. She watched their feet, her white athletic shoes trying to keep pace with his shiny black wing tips. Every few steps she gave him a glance. He never looked back. Rather he kept his eyes narrowed on the terminal ahead, his expression hard, the citadel of his feelings—if, indeed, he had any feelings—impregnable.

Inside the terminal Aiden draped his garment bag over a seat and set his briefcase on the floor. "Watch my things for me?"

Jill nodded and took a seat as he walked off to the ticket counter.

The Wellington airport conducted a brisk commuter service at this time of day, catering mostly to business people flying to Hartford or Albany or New York, which was Aiden's destination today. For longer flights, Aiden flew out of Logan International, but whenever possible, he opted for the smaller, more convenient airport.

Aiden slipped his ticket into his inside jacket pocket and returned to where Jill was sitting. He took the seat beside her. For a while they said nothing—like strangers traveling to different destinations, she thought. Her throat began to tighten.

Aiden was the first to break the silence. "Listen, Jill, when I get back, things are going to start moving fast and furiously, and despite our best intentions to remain amicable, hard feelings are bound to arise. So I just want to say now that I never meant for this to happen. When we got married, I meant till death do us part."

Jill nodded, staring at her knees, her eyes hot and gritty and threatening to brim over. Unexpectedly, he touched his hand to her cheek and gently turned her to face him. Even more unexpectedly, she leaned into the touch.

"I'm sorry I couldn't change for you," he whispered.

Couldn't? Jill thought. Had he even tried?

Reminded, her heart hardened, and she eased away from his touch. "I'm not angry, just sad that it's come to this."

"So am I. We had a lot of potential." With a sigh he sat back, away from her, and the brief emotional connection between them broke. "But, as you've often said, we're two very different people. We want different things out of life. No one's to blame."

Jill wasn't so sure about that, but she didn't want to start arguing again. "It's better this way, while Maddy's still too young to understand and be hurt."

"Yes, you're right." As always, he readily agreed with her. His eagerness to be done with their marriage hurt.

A voice over the public address system announced that Aiden's flight was boarding. Jill felt a sinking sensation in the pit of her stomach.

"You'd better be going."

"Yes." Aiden pulled himself out of his chair. She got to her feet, too. They were both frowning.

"Do you have your tie?" she asked out of habit.

He patted one pocket, then another. "Uh-huh." He glanced toward the line of passengers filing through the door that led outside to the waiting thirty-seater. An uneasy pause settled between them.

Usually he kissed her before leaving, but he wouldn't kiss her today. Usually he said he'd call, but there would be no more calls. It was over. Suddenly an overwhelming misery invaded her heart.

No, she wouldn't break down now. This wasn't the right place, wasn't the right time. She pulled in a deep breath, exhaled slowly and told herself she felt stronger.

The last passenger stepped through the door, and the

desk clerk gave Aiden a warning wave. Aiden nodded and returned his gaze to Jill. "Well, I really have to run." He lifted his bag from the chair and his briefcase from the floor. "You'll be all right?"

"Yes, of course." Jill smiled forcibly.

He took a backward step, his eyes sweeping over her, and for a second she thought she finally saw an unguarded emotion in them. Regret.

Fearing she might do something embarrassing, she quickly said, "Goodbye, Aiden."

He pressed his lips together in a hard, grim line, gave her a nod and turned. A moment later he was gone. Desolation streamed through her.

The ticket agent peeked up from the newspaper spread out on his desk, sympathy mingling with his curiosity. Jill lifted her chin, squared her shoulders and walked to the floor-to-ceiling window that looked out on the airfield. Aiden was just jogging up the stairs to the plane now, his dark hair glistening in the morning sun, suit jacket flapping, red tie tumbling out of his pocket and being caught with one-handed élan. Above him at the door, the flight attendant laughed and said something Jill couldn't hear but understood in a part of her that was deep and primal and totally female.

Aiden in the morning, on his way to New York. Was there ever such a sight? She pressed one palm to the window as if in doing so she might take one last touch of him, his beauty, his confidence, his drive. But then he stepped inside the plane and disappeared from view. "Goodbye, Aiden," she whispered. She lowered her hand and slipped it into the pocket of her jacket. A chapter of her life was over.

She ought to leave, she thought. She ought to do her grocery shopping and get home to relieve Mrs. O'Brien. Maybe she should call her mother, too, and fill her in on what was happening.

Jill groaned. She wanted to talk to her mother yet

dreaded the possibility of hearing those four painful words, "I told you so."

The doors of the plane closed, and the engines began their powerful, escalating whine. As Jill looked on, her mind drifted back three years to the evening she'd called home to say she was getting married.

"But, Jill, who *is* he, besides your boss?" Even now she could hear the doubt in her mother's voice. "Can you honestly say you know him after only two months of dating?"

Of course she knew him. Aiden Morse was the most attractive, most dynamic, most respected and intelligent man she'd ever met.

"But where is he from? What's his background?"

Jill told her mother what she knew, which wasn't a lot but which certainly should've satisfied her: that he was originally from Oregon, an only child, and his parents were both deceased. He'd come east for college and stayed on after graduation because he'd been offered a good job with the electronics firm where he'd done a student internship.

"But, Jill, he must have somebody," Mildred Kruger persisted when she learned no one from Oregon would be coming to the wedding. Family was a big issue with Jill's mother. "Who are his people?"

"Who cares?" Jill answered in mild exasperation—mild, because she was too much in love to argue. "I'm marrying the man, not his family."

Jill's gaze was fixed on the plane, on the dazzle of sunlight glinting off the fuselage. But her thoughts remained focused inward, on a day not long after her wedding when her mother began angling for grandchildren and Jill was forced to set her straight.

"Oh, Jill! Did you know he didn't want children?"

Yes, Jill had known. Aiden had always been honest with her about that, right from the beginning.

And then, of course, her mother had come back with,

"What sort of man doesn't want children?" With a husband as family oriented as Jill's father was, Mildred really couldn't envision any other sort.

Jill tried to explain. Children just didn't fit into Aiden's scheme of things. He was aiming for the top of the corporate ladder at ABX Industries, and he wanted to get there by the age of thirty-five. That was the year Greg Simmons, the president and CEO, planned to retire. Aiden simply didn't have the time to invest in children. As one of ABX's busiest vice presidents, he often worked twelve-hour days and spent as much time away on business as he did at home. His concern, Jill assured her mother, was not the effect children would have on him but the effect he'd have on them; he thought kids deserved more than he could give.

Jill could've explained Aiden's other reason for not wanting children, the fact that he'd spent his youth ping-ponging between his parents, who'd been divorced, and that he didn't have many happy memories of childhood. But she didn't. She thought that might paint too negative a picture of him.

And so, when her mother said she still didn't understand, Jill replied, "Lots of people don't want kids, Mom. They're content simply to be married, to enjoy their spouse, travel with them, entertain, have a nice home. Why is it so hard for you to accept that Aiden is one of them?"

Even now, three years later, her mother's answer still cut to the sensitive heart of the issue. "Because he's married to you."

At the time Jill had resented her mother's implication that, in agreeing to a childless marriage, she was doing something against her nature. Sure, she'd always loved children and foreseen herself as a mother, but she was certain she had adjusted. She was certain she'd embraced Aiden's vision.

And maybe she had. For a year, she'd been blissfully

happy. Although Aiden was an emotionally reserved man, careful to keep people at a distance, he showed none of that reserve with her, at least not in their love-making. In fact, his passion positively blinded her.

Their life was wonderful in other ways, too. They traveled to Hawaii on their honeymoon, to St. Thomas five months later, to Paris six months after that. They bought their house, a large Colonial that had once been featured in the life-styles section of the local paper. She worked as his private assistant, traveling with him on business trips. She played hostess at home to other executives and their wives. It seemed a wonderful life.

But then she got pregnant—and their wonderful life caved in.

The problem was she was happy, and she thought Aiden would be, too. She thought a year of married life had mellowed him and perhaps changed his outlook. In her private moments before telling him her news, she even let herself imagine him celebrating the unexpected turn of events. She saw him sweeping her up and whooping in joy. She saw him popping a bottle of champagne—as her father had done at the announcement of each of her mother's three pregnancies; as her brother had done, as well, when his wife got pregnant.

Unfortunately Aiden wasn't her father or her brother. If she lived to be a hundred, Jill would never forget how his face blanched when she told him.

"You're pregnant?"

"Yes."

"But... How did it happen?" It seemed all he wanted to do at first was lay blame.

When she confessed she thought she'd messed up with her birth control pills, his color came surging back. If there was one thing Aiden Morse couldn't abide, it was ineptitude.

"Did you do this on purpose, Jill?"

She was stunned. "Why would I do that?"

"Who knows?" he snapped angrily. "Maybe you wanted to slow me down."

"That's ridiculous. And anyway, who's at fault isn't important, Aiden. The question now is, what are we going to do about it?"

"Do? There's nothing *to* do. I wish it didn't exist, but it does, and so we can only go on from here."

Jill was relieved. At least he hadn't asked her to terminate the pregnancy. That would've ended their marriage right then and there. But he hadn't, and she clung to the hope that in time he'd adjust. The idea of becoming a father had been foisted on him unexpectedly, but in time, after the shock of her news wore off, he'd see it wasn't such a frightening prospect. As her pregnancy progressed, maybe he'd even become excited.

But it never happened.

Granted, he acted like an expectant father, in a superficial way, when in the company of others, but alone, at home, he shut down, retreating into his den and into himself. He didn't go shopping with Jill for the crib or layette, didn't read the child-care books she gave him, and didn't join her in Lamaze class. One of her friends became her birth partner instead. What he did do was begin traveling without her, and he began traveling a lot.

Still, she didn't give up hope. Time, that was all he needed, she thought, trying to ignore her mounting loneliness and sense of being deserted. Once he saw his newborn, she was sure he'd change. How could he not?

But he didn't even see his newborn until she was four days old. He was away on business. And in the months since, he'd only retreated farther and deeper into himself, getting more involved with his work and his colleagues. He'd never changed a diaper, never fed his daughter a bottle, and rarely ever held her.

Now the question wasn't, what sort of man doesn't want children? It was, how could a man not want his own child once it was born? For this, Jill had no answer.

For this, she'd run out of understanding and patience. And she was finally facing the truth of the matter, that her mother had been right. She'd married a man she didn't know: a selfish man, interested only in his own career goals; a rigid man, unable to change or grow; a distrustful man, guarding himself against any real intimacy; a cold man, one who could make love with staggering passion, yet didn't know how to love. Jill had given him time and innumerable chances to prove himself otherwise—a year and nine months, to be exact—but matters were only going from bad to worse.

Jill stood a little taller as she watched the airplane from the window and listened to the roar of its jets. She'd made the right decision, then, no doubt about it. She was tired of the loneliness, tired of feeling unloved, and she was downright furious at the damage he was doing to Maddy by ignoring her.

Daughters needed the love and attention of their fathers. Jill knew that from personal experience, remembering the confidence and sense of self-worth her father had fostered in her. She knew it, too, from the child-care books she read. Aiden was falling down on the job, big time, and didn't even care.

The small commuter plane taxied out to the runway and turned into takeoff position. Relief began to trickle through Jill's tensed body like warm honey. Yes, this was right. She was still young. Just twenty-six. Maybe in time she'd meet someone nice, someone who'd make her and Maddy his first priority, someone who didn't want to be president of his company at thirty-five, or fifty-five, or any age.

Maddy deserved a father who loved her, and Jill longed to have a husband, a real husband—partner and mate. She wouldn't care whether he was rich or poor, handsome or homely, just as long as he shared himself with her, his time, conversation, activities. His heart. That was what was important in life. The little things.

But if she never found anyone, that would be all right, too. She'd survive, and so would her daughter. Jill intended to shower Maddy with so much love, she'd never feel the lack of a second parent.

The plane began its run, landing gear rumbling on the tarmac, engines whining ever higher. *Yes, go, Aiden,* she thought as the plane thrust forward with increasing velocity. *Go chase your selfish dreams. I don't care anymore. Maddy and I are far better off without you.* Roaring down the runway, the plane lifted into the air. *All I want is to find peace of mind and put my life back together.*

The plane rose higher, climbing the air, catching the morning sun on its wings. And as she watched, Jill found herself relaxing into even deeper relief. It was over. The ordeal of breaking up was finished. She smiled.

She was about to turn from the window when she noticed the rising aircraft execute a strange little wobble in the air. She paused, curious, but after a while decided whatever she'd seen was just in her imagination.

The plane lifted over the far woods, and she was about to turn away once more. But then the wings did that tilting back-and-forth dance again, and her breath seized up on her. Something wasn't right with that takeoff. In fact, it suddenly seemed quite wrong.

Aiden tensed. He'd suspected something was wrong even before the plane left the ground. Now, as it lifted over the trees of Wellington, he was sure of it. Looking out the window on his right, he watched the horizon drop and rise, drop and rise. His fingers curled around the armrests of his seat, seeking something solid and steady to hang on to.

"What the hell?" the passenger beside him muttered.

Aiden tried to clear his mind. He'd traveled in all sorts of weather, through ice storms and thunder and gale-force winds. Today was beautiful. Nothing to worry about. Nothing.

The plane began to bank and, strangely, didn't stop until it had made a complete turn. "What the hell?" the man beside him grumbled again. To his own dismay, Aiden was thinking the same thing. By then, everyone on the plane was grumbling, some voices rising in anger, most in alarm.

The pilot came on the intercom, his deep, reassuring voice explaining they were heading back to the airport. He didn't say why, and no one was reassured, least of all Aiden. He recognized a bluff when he heard one.

"Keep your seat belts fastened," the pilot instructed. "I'll bring us in as smoothly as I can." Aiden heard the unspoken "but" in the pilot's voice and waited for him to continue, but apparently that was all he intended to say. The connection to the cockpit broke, leaving Aiden sitting amid a planeful of confused and frightened passengers.

He looked out the window and realized they were flying more wobble-winged than ever. He closed his eyes and took several slow breaths. Gripping the armrests, he forced his eyes open again. The plane had leveled off, but that did little to ease his anxiety. He could see the airfield ahead, the tops of the trees below. He measured the distance, to the airfield, to the trees—and a film of perspiration broke out on his face.

He wasn't a man who frightened easily, and he never ever panicked. But right now his mind was screaming—and alternately blanking out—and if that wasn't panic...

Unexpectedly he felt he had to get out of his seat. He had to get up. There was something he needed to do. Something urgent. He reached for the belt buckle, then foggily realized that that wasn't right: he had to stay strapped in. A bead of sweat trickled down his cheek.

The plane began to plough through the treetops, branches cracking and shearing and flying like matchsticks. Some of the passengers around him were crying; others, like him, were just numb. Oh, God, it was happening. Something terrible was coming. Something unspeakable. The knowledge was rising in him like floodwater, robbing him of breath, choking him.

He had to get out of this seat. He couldn't let it happen.

Abruptly the trees disappeared, and the plane shot out over the airfield. It was coming in for a landing. No, not coming in, *falling* in, too fast, much too fast, like a train out of control.

Frantic, Aiden craned his neck and peered toward the front of the plane, his gaze searching, searching…for what? His eyes throbbed. His ears hurt. Ah, yes, now he remembered.

Oh, God, he shouldn't have let her out of his sight. It was coming. Where was she? Where…

The plane hit the runway then, hard. The impact threw Aiden one way, then another, bashing him against the window wall repeatedly. Pain tore through him—his arm, his ribs, his leg. In a voice made raw by pain and guilt, he called out "Becky!" just before everything went black.

CHAPTER TWO

STANDING at the window inside the terminal, Jill watched in horrified numbness as the out-of-kilter plane hit the runway and went bumping and skidding along. Even behind the thick glass, she could hear the sickening screech of metal, the horrible bawling of the engines. The right wing dipped, grazing the tarmac and sending up a spray of friction sparks. Jill blanched as the image of fire exploded in her mind.

Finally, several hundred yards down the runway, the airplane ground to a stop and went ominously silent.

People had been gathering at the window for some time and now pressed all around her, their voices raised in alarm. Out on the airfield, an emergency vehicle suddenly raced toward the plane, which lay on its side like a felled behemoth.

Adrenaline rushed through Jill, freeing her from her dazed immobility. She turned from the window and, without a thought to what she was doing, bolted for the door.

"Hey, hey, hey." An arm shot out in front of her. "You can't go out there, miss."

Furious, Jill shot a glance at the person obstructing her way. A security guard. "My husband is on that plane," she said self-righteously.

"Calm down, calm down." The man's arms tightened around her. Only then did Jill realize she was fighting him. "I've worked here thirty years. This isn't serious. Not bad at all. People've walked away from a lot worse." The security guard pointed with his chin. "See? What did I tell you?"

Jill stopped resisting and followed the man's gaze. Sure enough, passengers were beginning to disembark from the plane, using an emergency chute out a mid-body door.

She emitted a strangled sigh of relief. As her limbs went limp, the guard let her go. Maybe it had only seemed like a serious crash because it was the only one she'd ever witnessed.

Barely breathing, she watched the chute, waiting for Aiden to appear. Meanwhile, airport personnel were quickly shepherding the passengers on the ground away from the plane. Others, dressed in gray overalls, were hosing down the fuselage with foam—to prevent fire, Jill thought. Alarm ripped through her with renewed force. *Please hurry, Aiden,* she implored silently. *Get out of that plane.*

A second airport vehicle, siren wailing, raced across the tarmac. This one was clearly an ambulance. When a third truck followed in its wake, Jill glowered at the security guard, sure he'd lied about the seriousness of the mishap.

Soon the area around the plane was crawling with airport workers. Even at a distance, their frenzied shouts and gestures carried to those watching at the window. Aiden was still nowhere to be found.

Another emergency door popped open. Stairs were rolled in place, and up went the overall-clad men, coming out an eternity later with passengers on stretchers. By then ambulances had arrived from the local hospital. Police cars, too. Wild-eyed, Jill searched the confusion on the field, looking for Aiden, feeling as if the entire universe was flying apart.

And then, all at once, there he was, surely one of the last to leave the plane. He was being helped down the stairs by a medic. Despite the distance separating them, Jill could see he was limping. But at least he was on his feet, upright and walking. She began to tremble in delayed reaction.

"May I have your attention, please?"

Distracted, Jill turned. A young woman who struck her as a secretary type was standing by the now-locked door to the airfield. She was clutching a clipboard to her chest, fingers squeezing so hard they were white.

"If there are any relatives or friends here of the passengers on the flight that just...just returned, I have some information. Everyone on the plane, regardless of injury, is being taken by ambulance to St. Luke's Hospital here in Wellington. Please don't try to get to them now or ride with them. That'll only slow things down. Go directly to the hospital. To Emergency. You can meet up with them there."

Jill already had her keys out of her bag and was racing for the door.

With a sudden influx of thirty patients, the ER at St. Luke's Hospital was chaotic. Jill paced the overcrowded waiting room for nearly an hour after giving her name at the desk. Patients were being triaged, she was told. At present the examining rooms could accommodate the relatives of only the most seriously injured. Well, that was something...

The wait also gave her time to complete Aiden's paperwork and then call home to Mrs. O'Brien, the babysitter. She also called ABX. Aiden's office needed to know what had happened and that he wouldn't be making his meeting in New York. Jill spoke directly to Greg Simmons, the head of the company. He asked her to keep him apprised.

Eventually a short, curly haired aide escorted Jill down the corridor to a room with four beds, four patients, one doctor and one too young nurse who looked on the verge of tears. Jill's gaze darted from bed to bed until she found the one where Aiden was lying, eyes closed. She hurried forward.

His beautiful suit had been removed, a blue hospital gown that barely reached his knees replacing it. "Oh, Aiden," she whispered sympathetically, the rancor of the past twenty-four hours momentarily put aside. Undressed and splayed out under the harsh hospital lights, he seemed so uncharacteristically helpless, so stripped of his dignity.

But as Jill's attention focused, she realized that stripped dignity was the least of Aiden's problems. His body was a mass of angry cuts and already purpling bruises.

The doctor swiveled from the adjacent bed. "Don't touch his arm, please. It's fractured."

Jill yanked back her extended hand. "Sorry." She hadn't noticed the splint before then. "Aiden, are you in any pain?"

He opened his eyes slowly, turned his head and gazed at her. His eyes, usually so alert and quick, seemed glassy and depthless.

"Aiden?" she asked uncertainly.

The doctor left the patient he'd been tending and joined her bedside. "Hi. I'm Dr. Costas."

"Jill Morse, Aiden's wife." She inclined her head toward her husband. "How is he?"

"Lucky. His injuries are minor. Those lacerations and contusions make it look worse than it is. We still have to take him to X ray, of course, but my guess is a simple fracture above the wrist."

"What about…at the airport I saw him limping."

"Yes. His left ankle is swollen. But if he was walking, it's probably just a sprain. Don't worry. We'll X-ray him thoroughly to be sure."

As if on cue, two orderlies entered the room. "You have a patient for X ray?" one of them asked.

"Yes. Just a moment." The doctor scribbled something on Aiden's chart.

Jill touched her fingers to Aiden's head, brushing gingerly at his hair. He looked at her, then looked around the room.

"Doctor, is he...all right?" She bit her lip.

"His disorientation? I was just about to get to that." The doctor slipped the chart into its holder at the foot of the bed. "I checked him for concussion but don't see any evidence of it. I could be wrong, and he will be reexamined by someone in neurology, but I believe he's just in a mild state of shock. Perfectly understandable, considering what he's been through."

Shock? Aiden? The two notions seemed mutually exclusive.

"Give him time to rest," the doctor added. "I'm sure he'll be more like himself in a few hours. Now, do you want to go to X ray with him?"

"Uh...oh, yes." Jill stepped aside as the two orderlies wheeled Aiden toward the door.

A couple of hours passed before the emergency department calmed sufficiently for Jill to meet in consultation with Dr. Costas again. Back in the four-bed examining room, the physician placed Aiden's X-ray films on a lighted panel and pointed out the fracture on his right forearm, which by now was set and safely encased in a plaster cast. He'd also had a few of his cuts sutured.

Jill stared at the lighted films, her eyes bleary from tension. "How long until his arm is healed?"

"Completely? Oh, approximately eight to ten weeks. Is he right-handed?"

"Yes." Jill grimaced, suddenly aware of what that meant. Aware, too, of the trick fate had played on her and Aiden on the verge of their separating.

"What sort of work does he do?"

"He's in management. A desk job basically."

"Oh. I never would've guessed from his strong build. Just as well. He can probably return to the office in a week or so. Lucky he's not a carpenter or a bricklayer."

"Yes." Jill glanced uncertainly at her husband. He was lying on the bed in the corner, eyes closed. So still.

"Right now, though, we're going to admit him for a couple of days." The doctor turned off the light and, as he gathered Aiden's X rays, explained, "It's airline policy. They don't want to be liable if any complications develop."

"I understand."

"Even if it weren't their policy, I'd suggest admitting him. He still isn't as alert as he should be. We'd like to keep an eye on that." The doctor slipped the films into a large manila envelope. "I just got word that a bed is ready. So with your permission..."

Jill sat by the window in Aiden's room until dinnertime, watching the sugar-and-water solution drip through his IV tube and the color of his bruises slowly darken and spread. In all that time the only words he spoke were *yes* and *no* in response to questions posed by the doctors and nurses who examined him. Quite often, Jill noticed, his answers were inappropriate or downright wrong.

Her shoulders ached with tension knots and her head throbbed, but everyone continued to reassure her the situation wasn't unusual. Aiden just needed quiet rest. Besides, he was on a painkiller, which contributed to his disorientation.

"Please go home," implored the young student nurse who came in to check Aiden's blood pressure at six o'clock. "Go see your baby and have a decent meal. He'll be fine."

Jill reluctantly complied. She certainly wasn't doing anyone any good here, and she did need to relieve Mrs. O'Brien. The poor woman had stayed with Maddy all day, and Jill would have to prevail upon her again tomorrow.

Jill approached her husband's bed. "Aiden?" He slowly opened his eyes. "I'll see you in the morning."

He gazed at her, looked around the room, met her eyes again and blinked.

"Try to rest. I'm sure you'll feel a lot better tomorrow." Then, because the nurse was still in the room and would expect such a gesture, Jill leaned forward and kissed Aiden's forehead. "See you first thing in the morning."

Aiden smiled faintly—peacefully, she thought—and closed his eyes.

Jill got home in just enough time to put Maddy to bed. The familiar routine was balm to her frazzled nerves. She gave her a quick bath, dressed her in a cozy, one-piece sleeper and, settling into the Salem rocker by the crib, hummed a lullaby while Maddy drank from her bottle.

This was Jill's favorite part of the day.

At a year old, Maddy was already walking, albeit unsteadily, and making a few sounds that Jill understood as words. In short, she was quickly growing into a self-propelled toddler. But at bedtime, she reverted to being Jill's baby, the warm little bundle she'd carried inside her for nine months, the infant who still needed to cuddle close to her mother's heart.

In the dim light cast from a calico-shaded lamp, Maddy's fine blond hair glowed like dandelion fuzz. Against the pad of Jill's index finger, her cheek felt like velvet. With the bottle only half empty, her delicate eyelids began to droop and soon her body lay slack.

Jill smiled, her heart overflowing with love for this little miracle who'd unexpectedly blessed her existence.

Maddy hadn't been planned, but now that she was here, Jill couldn't imagine life without her.

As always her thoughts turned to Aiden. How much he was missing. After the day's events, she couldn't be angry, though, just melancholy. This was his daughter, too, his flesh and blood. Why couldn't he see how delightful she was, how smart, how beautiful and affectionate? Why couldn't he love her? He said he did, but saying didn't make it so, and actions spoke louder than words.

Jill hugged Maddy closer, as if shielding her from Aiden's cold dispassion, and pressed a kiss to her downy-soft hair.

But, of course, it didn't matter anymore what Aiden felt toward their daughter. Soon he would be out of her life—out of both their lives. She'd nearly forgotten. The confusion and high emotion of the plane accident had pushed their impending separation out of her thoughts. But now it was coming back, the full brunt.

She laid Maddy in her crib, covered her with a pink blanket her mother had crocheted, and turned off the light. Out in the hall she was tempted to retreat to her own room and fall into bed for the night. But she hadn't eaten yet and knew she had to keep up her strength. She doubted she'd sleep anyway. She only *wanted* to sleep, to blank out this painful day and escape into unconsciousness.

Jill tiptoed downstairs to the kitchen and warmed a can of chicken noodle soup. Her appetite was gone, though, another casualty of her anxiety. After eating only half the bowl and two crackers, she gave it up.

She called home to Ohio and filled her parents in on Aiden's misadventure, telling them not to worry, his injuries were minor. They were worried anyway, both asking questions at once from separate phone extensions. Jill decided to omit telling them about her and Aiden's decision to break up. One piece of bad news seemed enough to handle for now. Besides, with his injuries, Aiden probably wouldn't be moving out for a few weeks. Time enough to tell them then.

Her mother offered to fly out, but Jill convinced her it wasn't necessary. After assuring her parents she'd call twice a day to keep them posted, she finally hung up the phone.

She slipped on a fleece jacket, opened the kitchen door and stepped out to the redwood deck at the back of the house. Immediately she was greeted with the nocturnal sound of peepers sending up their exuberant chorus from the boggy woods. Dropping into a chaise longue, she smiled faintly. Peepers. That was one of her favorite spring sounds, right up there with the song of robins.

Unexpectedly Jill's eyes burned. Instead of being filled with hope and joy as she usually was in spring, she felt absolutely miserable. She closed her eyes and two hot tears squeezed through her lashes.

What a day! First, the decision to get a divorce, and then the plane accident. What a long, wretched, miserable day!

Jill was startled out of her dark thoughts by the ringing of the telephone. Swiping at her cheeks, she got off the chaise and hurried back into the kitchen.

"Hello?" she answered, trying not to sound nasally.

"Jill? I just heard."

Jill closed the door and the sound of the peepers died. "Hi, Eric." She turned on the overhead lights and sank into the chair at the phone desk.

"Are you all right?" Her neighbor's voice carried a gratifying measure of worry.

"Oh, I'm holding up," she replied, shrugging off her jacket.

"Tell me all about it."

And she did. For the next ten minutes Jill poured out the happenings of the day. As usual, Eric listened attentively, occasionally murmuring sympathetic noises.

She'd met Eric a year ago, after Maddy was born, those late spring days when Jill used to take her for walks in her carriage. Eric, a divorced real-estate agent and avid gardener with custody of his six-year-old son, lived a few streets away.

Gardening was the thing that initially drew them. Jill would always slow down when she got to his property because his front yard flower beds were such a delight. Since he was often working in those flower beds when she came by, they began to talk, sharing gardening tips, and then cuttings, and eventually visits to each other's yards.

The second thing that drew them was the children. She loved her daughter, he loved his son, and that alone was enough to forge a friendship. They swapped parental anecdotes, gave each other advice, and because Eric's work hours were erratic, Jill began occasionally minding his son after school.

"I'm glad Aiden got through it okay," Eric said when Jill had finished telling him about the crash. "Not everyone was that lucky. Did you watch the news this evening?"

"No. I haven't had the chance."

"One of the passengers didn't make it. Had a fatal heart attack on the way to the hospital. Several people are in intensive care, too. On the critical list."

Although the crash was in the past, Jill tensed as if it still had the power to reach out and harm Aiden. Alarm in retrospect, she supposed. "I didn't realize it was that serious."

"Do you want me to come over? I just put Brady to bed, but I can get a baby-sitter."

"No, you stay put. I'm pretty tired. I'll probably be going to bed soon myself."

"Well, if you change your mind..."

"I won't."

The line hummed with taut silence for a moment. In a far more confidential voice, Eric said, "Did you and Aiden have your talk?"

Jill fingered a pen, turning it end over end. "Yes."

"And?"

She gazed at a small framed photograph on the desk—her and Aiden on their honeymoon. They were sitting by a waterfall, colorful leis about their necks, their arms around each other. For a moment she remembered their happiness, not with her mind but with her heart.

The next instant a shaft of guilt speared through her. She felt as if she'd betrayed Aiden by discussing their private affairs with this man.

She gave herself a firm mental shake, remembering that Eric wasn't just any man. He was a friend, perhaps the best she had. Furthermore, he'd detected she was having marital problems long before she'd confided in him, and she'd confided in him only because he'd spent considerable time in family counseling when his own marriage was in trouble. Jill had thought he might be able to help.

As it turned out, nothing had helped, but at least he'd provided an outlet for her anxiety and unhappiness and indecision. Eric had also opened her eyes to the injustice Aiden was perpetrating against her and had given her the courage to look out for herself and her child.

Shakily she answered, "We agreed to separate."

A long sigh crackled over the line. "I can't say that I'm not relieved, Jill. You deserve a better life."

She dropped her head to her hand. Eric was right, she knew he was, but she really preferred not talking about it tonight. She was weary right to the bone, and somehow it didn't seem appropriate talking about Aiden while he lay in the hospital.

After a while Eric added, "I know you must be upset after the day you've had, but you really ought to get in touch with a lawyer. As soon as possible, too. Take it from someone who's been there."

Jill massaged her throbbing temples. "Aiden asked me to wait, so we could see our lawyer together."

"That's a great way to lose your shirt, Jill. Mark Hillman is *Aiden's* friend."

Jill opened her mouth, wanting to defend Aiden, wanting to say he wasn't grasping and vindictive the way Eric's ex-wife had been. But maybe Eric had a point. Aiden had proved to be a lot of things she hadn't counted on.

"Do you have a recommendation?"

He chuckled. "Sure. The man-eater who represented my ex. Would you like me to contact her for you?"

"Oh, I'm not sure, Eric."

"I know. It's been a difficult day and you probably don't want to think about lawyers right now. But I wouldn't be making a commitment or anything, just calling to see if she has time to take you on."

"Well," Jill vacillated, "I suppose it wouldn't hurt."

"Of course, it wouldn't. I'll give her a call first chance I get." After a pause, "Mind if I ask another question?" Without waiting, he said, "What are you planning to do about Aiden's convalescence?"

"I've been trying not to think about that, either."

"Are you going to let him come home when he's released from the hospital?"

Jill sat up straighter, frowning. "Where else would he go?"

"His arm is only broken, Jill."

"His ankle is sprained, too, and he has some terrible bruises. Very painful."

"That doesn't mean you have to play nursemaid. Hell, he can hire a home health aide. The aide can do everything, probably even drive him to work."

"Sure, after he's recovered a bit. But I'm not going to put him out on the street first day home from the hospital. That'd be uncivilized."

"He wouldn't be out on the street. He could move into a furnished apartment."

He probably could, Jill thought. In fact, he'd already mentioned moving back to Shawmut Gardens, and she seemed to recall those apartments being furnished.

"Living under the same roof after you've already agreed to a divorce is going to get mighty uncomfortable, Jill. You'll probably be at each other's throats."

It was a depressing thought, too depressing, because Eric was probably right.

"Well, I just thought I'd mention it, give you something to think about."

"Yes, I'll think, I promise. Right after I get some sleep."

"Okay. Sorry for keeping you up. See you soon, Jill."

"Thanks for calling."

"Hey, Jill?"

"Yes?"

"Hang in. It's all up from here."

She replaced the receiver in its cradle and frowned at it for several thoughtful minutes. All up from here? Then why did she feel she was on a greased slide, heading nowhere but down?

The hospital was still in the throes of its early morning routine when Jill stepped off the elevator at Aiden's floor the next morning. Breakfast trays rattled by on food carts. Doctors and nurses were making their rounds, and candy-stripers were delivering flowers. Through this bustle Jill made her way to Aiden's room, wondering if she was too early, if perhaps she'd be in the way.

But when she got to his door, she discovered his room was quiet. The bed had already been made, and Aiden was alone. She stood on the threshold unnoticed and marveled at the difference in him from yesterday.

Granted, his arm was still in its cast, his ankle was still bandaged, and his bruises were still quite ugly. But he was up, sitting in a chair, sipping coffee and reading the *New York Times*. His hair was neatly combed in its customary side-parted fashion and, although a day's growth of beard shaded his face, she could see that his color was back.

So, everyone had been right after all, she thought. The only thing he'd needed was a good night's rest to shake off the trauma of yesterday's misadventure.

"Good morning!" she sang with undisguised relief. "Aiden, you're looking wonderful today!"

Aiden glanced up, his eyes sharp as ever. "Thank you," he said politely, his gaze moving over her slowly and carefully, "Jill."

It struck her as odd, the way he tacked on her name.

She stepped further into the room, coming to pause at the bed, where she placed her purse. "How's your arm today?"

Aiden folded the newspaper as best he could and tossed it on the long, wide windowsill where several floral arrangements were on display. "Achy, but nothing I can't live with." He resumed studying her, every inch, every eye-blink. You'd think he'd never seen her before. His scrutiny made her unaccountably edgy.

"Do you need a painkiller?"

"They don't want to give me anything like that today. They say it might confuse things." For some reason he found that funny.

Frowning in deepening puzzlement, Jill stepped

around the bed and approached the window. "You have so many flowers already. Who are they from?"

Aiden shrugged. "People at work, I think."

"You think?" She turned to look at him, wondering if he was joking. If he was, she couldn't see the humor in it.

He swallowed. "Sorry. I'm trying to remember..."

Her blood began to slow and chill.

"Mrs. Morse?" A doctor swung into the room just then, slightly out of breath. He was tall, wiry and perhaps in his late fifties. He had a balding pate and a closely trimmed gray beard.

Jill somehow croaked out a yes.

"Hi, I'm Dr. Grogan. I just called your house, but the woman there told me you were already on your way. I was hoping...may I have a word with you out in the corridor?"

Jill glanced at Aiden, resisting the alarm that was beginning to rise in her.

"Take these seats," Aiden suggested, getting up and fitting a crutch under his arm. "I was just about to go take a shower, anyway." He hobbled past them, his eyes flicking over Jill again. At the door a nurse met him and escorted him to the shower room down the corridor.

"What's going on?" Jill asked, taking the seat Aiden had vacated.

"Your husband... Well, let me start at the beginning." The doctor settled into the chair beside hers. "Aiden awoke early this morning alert and hungry. The nurse on duty was quite pleased. The fog he was in yesterday seemed a thing of the past."

"But...?" Jill prodded, holding her breath.

"But it soon became apparent to her he was having difficulty remembering certain things. He had no idea where he was or why he was here. He didn't even know *who* he was."

Jill gazed into the doctor's clinically impassive eyes, looking for hidden meanings, because what he was saying verbally certainly made no sense. "Was Aiden's head injured? Was something overlooked yesterday? A cousin of mine once had a concussion, and for several days she was terribly confused and forgetful."

"No, there's no sign of physical head injury. What we seem to be dealing with here, Mrs. Morse, is a dissociative disorder."

"A dissociative...?"

"A case of psychogenic amnesia."

Jill clutched the arms of her chair, trying to brake the sudden dreamlike sensation of falling. "Amnesia?" she repeated hollowly.

"Yes, brought on by the trauma of the plane accident."

She shook her head. "This isn't happening. This..."

"I know. It's difficult news first thing in the morning. What's worse is, Aiden seems to have total amnesia. That's unusual."

Jill covered her mouth with her hand to keep it from quivering.

"The good news is, the prognosis for a quick and full recovery is excellent. Amnesia patients rarely lose their memory for long. In fact, just in the short time that I was examining Aiden this morning, several blocks of memory fell back into place. College years, I believe. I wouldn't be at all surprised if the rest followed within days."

Jill looked at the gray-bearded doctor more closely. "Are you a psychiatrist?"

He nodded. "Sorry. I should've mentioned that."

In spite of her numbness, Jill had the presence of mind to ask, "Have you treated any other patients with this disorder?"

"Several." He then explained he was something of a

regional expert on memory disorders. He was on staff here at St. Luke's and a few other hospitals, and he also had a private practice in Boston. Jill felt somewhat better knowing Aiden was in good hands.

"Luckily, I was here this morning, checking on one of my patients. I was able to see Aiden and run a few diagnostic tests."

Jill exhaled shakily. "And you say he's forgotten everything?"

"Not exactly everything. His knowledge-and-skills memory is still intact, as well as his priming and associative memory." He paused, realizing he'd lost Jill. "For instance, he remembers how to read and write. That he takes his coffee black and combs his hair from right to left. He remembers his times tables, his manners, and I'm quite sure that if he was a basketball player before the accident, he still has the ability to hit a jumpshot now. He's just lost his episodic memory, his memory of life events, the people he knows, his personal circumstances."

"He realizes he's married to me," Jill offered hopefully.

"Yes. Because one of the nurses told him. He also knows his name, his occupation, and the fact that he was on a plane that went down yesterday, because he was inadvertently given the information. He can learn things, Mrs. Morse. His short-term memory is functioning fine. But that isn't the same as remembering them."

Jill fought against a trembling that started in her midsection and spread right to the roots of her hair. "He really doesn't remember me?"

The doctor shook his head sympathetically. "Sorry."

"Oh, I don't feel bad for myself. It's Aiden. I can't imagine him not being in full command. It must be terrifying to be cut adrift from all your memories." Well, *she* would be terrified. Aiden, she realized, was probably impatient.

"It is an unsettling circumstance, although your husband is being remarkably philosophical about it."

"Aiden?" Jill's eyebrows lifted.

"Yes." The doctor smiled as if at a private joke. "He told me he feels light, floaty, as though a burden's been lifted off his shoulders. He wanted to know how much Demerol we'd slipped him."

Jill didn't return the doctor's smile. She was wondering if *she* was the burden Aiden had referred to and if forgetting their marriage was the reason he felt light.

"Try not to worry," the physician said, misinterpreting her frown. "His memory will come back."

"Are you sure?"

"There are never any ironclad guarantees, but I'm fairly sure. It'll just take time."

"How much time?"

"That, I can't predict. But if the situation lingers, I can help it along with either hypnosis or a drug called Sodium Amytol. That is, if you'd like me to assume his case."

"Yes, I think I would."

The doctor nodded agreeably. "For now, though, I'd prefer to let nature take its course in its own good time. That almost always works."

Jill pressed her lips together in what she hoped was a smile. "Will you keep him here until he's fully recovered, then?"

"Oh, no. I'm afraid insurance won't allow that. We'll keep him for three or four days, as planned, but beyond that..." Dr. Grogan shook his head. "He isn't physically ill, nor is he a danger to himself or anyone else, and I can treat him as well in my office as I can here. If he didn't have a home and family to return to, of course,

I'd try to keep him hospitalized. But he does have a home, and that makes a world of difference."

Jill's gaze darted nervously.

"Is anything wrong, Mrs. Morse?"

"Um, as a matter of fact, yes. My husband and I...we recently decided to...to separate."

"Oh. When I read his address, I assumed he was still living at home."

"He is. We didn't decide to break up until a couple of days ago."

"Ah, I see."

Ah, he saw what? Jill wondered in sudden paranoia. She studied the doctor's face, but it was even more impassive than Aiden's usually was.

"Is there someone else he can be released to?"

"Not really. He has no other family in the area."

Dr. Grogan rubbed a hand over his mouth, considering. "Will his returning home present too awkward a situation for you?"

Fragments of Jill's conversation with Eric returned to haunt her. She was loathe to admit it, but she'd awakened this morning with the intention of asking Aiden to consider moving to an apartment when he was released. She stared at her knees, unable to meet the doctor's eyes. How could anyone expect Aiden to go anywhere but home now?

"No," she said in a thin voice. "Of course he can come home."

"Good, because he'll recover a lot faster there among familiar surroundings. They'll trigger associations, and those will trigger others, and before you know it..."

Just then the nurse who'd escorted Aiden to the shower room appeared at the door. "Doctor, Mr. Morse will be returning shortly."

"Thanks. We're just about done here, anyway."

"Should I stay?" Jill asked, half hoping to be sent home. "Or will my presence just frustrate him?"

"Stay, by all means. A familiar face can only help. But one word of advice. Don't tell him you and he are breaking up. He seemed relieved to learn he was married and had someone to help him through this. Actually, don't tell him anything at all, if you can help it. It's important for him to remember things on his own."

"I'll try," Jill said, frowning, "but I can't guarantee I won't slip."

"Of course. And you'll find there are things you'll have to tell him. All I'm saying is, don't make a career of it. Educating him won't do him a bit of good. He has to unlock those doors himself."

Aiden stepped into the room. Instead of the fragrance of his usual expensive aftershave, he smelled of hospital soap. Jill made a mental note to bring his toiletries from home. And his housecoat. He was wearing a thin hospital robe that had definitely seen better days.

"Aiden," the doctor said, rising, "I'll stop by at the end of my rounds to see if you need anything. Until then, your wife is going to keep you company. Okay?"

Faced with being alone with Aiden, Jill tensed. He undoubtedly hated this situation. He hated any sort of vulnerability. He was going to be short with himself and with everyone around him.

Aiden's eyes moved apprehensively from the doctor to Jill.

"She understands you don't remember her. You don't have to pretend that you do."

Jill noticed Aiden swallow, his fingers tighten around the sash of his bathrobe. Inexplicably her dread of sitting with him began to slacken.

The doctor shook hands with Jill, gave her his office number in case she had any questions, and then said goodbye.

Finally alone, she and Aiden looked at each other warily.

"This is very strange," Aiden confessed with a tight smile.

"Yes, it is." Jill clutched her arms, rubbing them as if she were cold.

"Everyone says we're married, so I guess we are, in which case—" his face took on an expression she couldn't recall ever seeing before "—I want to say I'm really and truly sorry for causing you this trouble."

Jill's eyes opened wide. "What?"

Thinking she hadn't heard him, he repeated his apology.

Again, his words caught her by surprise. Aiden so rarely apologized. "Aiden, you're the one who suffered the accident. There's no need to be sorry."

"Sure there is. You must be worried, and I'm the reason. It's all so unnecessary, too. And embarrassing," he added with a wry twist of his lips. "A broken arm is one thing. I can live with that. But losing my memory because I'm repressing the crash?" He shook his head. "That seems downright cowardly of me, don't you think?"

Jill's mouth dropped open. Aiden wasn't normally into humor of the self-deprecating sort.

"I mean," he continued, "are any of the other passengers repressing? Not that I've heard. I'm the only one who seems unable to face the music."

He paused. Apparently she looked uneasy because he said, "Sorry. I'm blathering." He pushed his hand through his damp hair in a familiar gesture and mumbled unfamiliarly, "Nervous, I guess."

He walked past her and looked out the window, missing Jill's amazement. She'd never seen him like this before, apologetic, thoughtful of others, humble. But then, he'd lost his memory. That would humble anyone, she supposed.

Still gazing out the window, Aiden murmured, "I must be putting you out. One of the nurses told me you...we have a small child." He turned, his gaze sweeping over her quickly, but there was no mistaking his male curiosity.

Heat bloomed in Jill's cheeks as she realized Aiden was probably trying to see himself with her, a virtual stranger, trying to imagine them making love, making a baby.

"Yes. Her name is Maddy," Jill replied as smoothly as she could. "Well, that's what we call her. Her full name is Madison. Madison Kay Morse." As soon as she'd said it, she remembered she shouldn't be furnishing Aiden the facts of his life.

Resting back on the sill, Aiden whistled softly. "Quite a mouthful."

"Yes, it is." She smiled fondly. "But she's showing every sign of growing into it."

"I wish I could..." He left off. Could? Could what? Remember her? "Where is she now?"

"At home with a baby-sitter."

"Ah."

Jill realized Aiden's eyes were on her again. She looked away, but her self-consciousness remained, her awareness of her body, her hair, her clothes. She wished she'd dressed with more care, but she hadn't known her husband would be looking at her with such intense interest today.

"Am I keeping you from work? Do you have a job you should be at? If you have to leave, I don't mind."

"No. I...I'm a stay-at-home mom."

"Ah." He still seemed a little embarrassed for not knowing something this basic about her. But then he smiled. "Good for you. Too many kids are being shuffled off to day-care these days. Don't you think?"

"Yes, I do." She just hadn't thought *he* had any opinion on the subject. "Would you like something to drink? Another cup of coffee?"

"Sure. I take it black, one sugar." He paused, his expression screwing up. "No. You know what I'd really like?" he confessed with a dimpled smile. "A tall glass of cold root beer."

Jill looked at him askance. "Since when do you like root beer?"

"Jill, I've always liked root beer." He spoke so readily that for a moment she doubted her own memory. Was this a facet of him she'd once known and forgotten?

No. She couldn't remember him ever expressing a fondness for soft drinks, any kind. But for now she'd humor him. "Root beer, it is. I'll be right back."

Still doubtful, she returned from the soda machine down the hall with a can of Hires. Her doubt vanished, though, when he popped the tab, took several swallows and sighed in deep satisfaction.

Jill stared at him, confounded by the man who'd awakened this morning in her husband's body. What she knew about amnesia could fit into a thimble, but it seemed to her that the loss of episodic memory would have little effect on one's basic personality.

But do you know him, Jill? her mother's voice badgered from a corner of her brain. *Who is he, really?* Jill gave the voice a dismissive shake.

Aiden moved aside a basket of flowers and hoisted himself onto the windowsill. He finished off the soda and set the can down. "So you're my wife."

She gulped and nodded, aware of his close perusal again.

His eyes glittered and a corner of his mouth lifted in

a grin that could only be called heart-stopping. "I've got good taste."

Jill's stomach did an unanticipated flip. Before she could regain her equilibrium, he leveled another unexpected remark her way.

"You have a small port-wine birthmark at the top of your right thigh."

After a stunned pause, Jill laughed. "Yes!"

"I just remembered."

"That's wonderful!" she exclaimed, ignoring her embarrassment at the nature of his memory. Of all things to remember about her! "Dr. Grogan said this would happen. I have to be honest, I was skeptical, but now I see he was right. You're going to be okay."

"Well, of course I am. Come sit. We have to talk some more."

CHAPTER THREE

IN SPITE of his optimism, Aiden recovered only a few other random memories during his stay at St. Luke's. While his lack of progress didn't seem to faze the hospital staff, it certainly worried Jill.

Her first concern was Aiden's health of course, but she was also worried about his job. Although amnesia was an unusual malady, and one she was constantly assured would pass, it was still a psychological disorder. People reacted strangely to psychological disorders, harboring unwarranted prejudices and fears. Even after he was well, Aiden's authority at work might be undermined. Confidence in his ability to perform might deteriorate, as well. She feared he might even find himself demoted or, worse, out of a job.

After a consultation with Dr. Grogan, Jill decided to keep the people at ABX uninformed about the full scope of Aiden's condition. When she called to give his office an update, she said his physical injuries were more complicated than they'd first appeared and he might have to stay out of work longer than anticipated. Dr. Grogan agreed that was the prudent course to take.

She didn't tell her friend Eric about Aiden's loss of memory, either. She wasn't sure why exactly. It certainly would've been easier on her to have someone she could share her problems and anxieties with. But for some reason it seemed more important to stand united with Aiden on this issue and keep him protected on all fronts. She supposed it was the extent of his vulnerability that made her feel that way.

"You mean, you're letting him come home?" Eric

asked, sitting in Jill's kitchen the third morning Aiden was in the hospital. He'd just seen his son off to school and decided to surprise Jill with a visit before going to work.

"I don't see what else I can do." Jill was beginning to get irked with Eric's lack of sympathy for Aiden. "Besides, I've been married to him for this long. What's a few more weeks?"

"You're going to be sorry. Guaranteed."

"Not as sorry as I'll be if I turn him out." She set two cups of coffee on the table and sat down.

Eric looked at her through the curls of steam rising from his cup. He was a good-looking man, of medium height and build, with sandy-brown hair, warm hazel eyes, and a face that was open and friendly.

"After all the heartache you've suffered because of him..." He pressed his lips together and shook his head in a disparaging manner. "Jill, don't tell me you still have feelings for Aiden."

"No, of course not. I just don't want the burden of a guilty conscience," she said. "I'm doing myself the favor. Now let's get off the subject."

But the truth of the matter was, Jill did feel something for Aiden. Pity most likely.

Not that he needed it. He was showing remarkable resiliency. With the aid of his crutch, he took long walks through different wards, often stopping to chat with other, less fortunate, patients. Instead of hospital gowns, he insisted on wearing regular clothing—comfortable jeans and sweatshirts—which he asked her to bring from home. Since he didn't own much casual clothing, she'd been forced to go shopping for him, a chore she'd rather enjoyed.

He played aggressive gin rummy with her, gloating when he won, grumbling when he lost, but all with a teasing attitude that told her he was really just having fun. He flirted with the older nurses, which earned him their good-natured scolding—as well as their extra attention. He was even able to joke about his amnesia.

No, Aiden wasn't moping about, pitying himself for his affliction. He was taking it with grace and humor. The last thing he needed was anyone's pity, least of all Jill's.

Or so she thought—until she walked into his room the evening before he was to be released.

He was standing at the window, one hand braced on the sill, shoulders hunched. Stepping closer, she saw he was watching the cars coming and going in the lit parking lot below. Although his gaze was fixed, it seemed unfocused, and the grooves on the sides of his mouth were deep.

Jill stood beside him, surprised by a sudden insight. "Are you afraid of leaving the hospital?" she asked softly.

"Yes," he said even more softly.

Jill's heart contracted at his admission. He'd been acting so cavalier about his condition, she'd come to believe it really didn't bother him. But of course it would. How frightening it must be to remember nothing, to reach with one's mind and find nothing to grasp. It must be like living suspended in an unending darkness, all sense of time and place and direction gone.

Jill was surprised to find she was frightened, too, but for a very different reason. She didn't know this man standing beside her. During the past couple of days, she'd spent considerable time visiting him, and he wasn't the Aiden she knew or remembered. What frightened her wasn't his strange new personality but rather the possibility she might actually get to like this version of him.

Aiden's gaze swept over the darkening landscape, and he sighed heavily. "I don't remember my way around," he said. "I should, but I don't. I don't recognize a damn thing out there." His voice betrayed an anguish he was trying to hide.

"It'll come back, Aiden." Jill lifted her hand and almost placed it on his back, but then thought better of the gesture. So far she'd managed to limit physical contact to only what was absolutely necessary.

He continued to stare out at the unfamiliar world. "It wouldn't matter if it didn't come back, if I had to learn each street and landmark as if I were visiting the town for the first time. I could live with that. What I can't live with is forgetting the people I'm supposed to be close to. It's beyond my comprehension how that can happen." His scowl deepened. "How can I not remember my own daughter?"

Jill bit her tongue, thinking he didn't have a whole lot of memories to draw from to begin with. He'd spent so little time with Maddy.

"How can I not remember you?" He turned to look at her, his gaze ardent, traveling the smooth sweep of her hair from the crown of her head to her shoulders. "I don't know where you came from or how we met, when our anniversary is or even what toppings you like on your pizza."

And you don't know that none of that matters anymore. Our marriage is ending, she thought guiltily.

"I'll tell you something strange, though." Aiden looked directly at her, right into her eyes—a new habit she found most disconcerting. "When I'm with you," he said, "I have a memory of love."

Jill stared at him, dumbfounded. "You what?"

He nodded. "The feeling isn't attached to any specific memory or incident. It's just something deep inside me, a vague sense of rightness about us, a sense of belonging."

Jill's breath suddenly seemed impossible to catch.

Aiden wasn't normally in the habit of expressing his feelings, any feelings, least of all romantic ones.

"When you arrive each day," he said, "I get warm here." Looking terribly sincere, he laid his left hand over his heart. But then a rakish grin lifted the corners of his mouth as he added, "And elsewhere."

Jill didn't know where to settle her gaze.

"And because of that," he continued, his expression sobering again, "I can cope with being lost. You're an anchor, Jill. I may be way out at sea without a compass, but as long as I have this memory of love, I know I'll be okay, and I want to go home."

Aiden's words plagued Jill for the rest of that night. Making up the hide-a-bed in the guest room, she wondered what he meant. *When I'm with you, I have a memory of love.* Where in heaven's name was that coming from?

Was it just a generalized physical attraction to her? Or was his "memory of love" more defined, an accumulated state of mind built from all the times they'd made love?

Jill was at a loss for answers. Maybe she could ask Dr. Grogan about it sometime.

Finished with the bed, she opened the window to let in some fresh air. Hearing the peepers, she lingered awhile, listening, watching the moonlight slide through the woods.

What worried her primarily, though, was Aiden's assumption about their relationship—that they were still a happily married couple. What did he expect of her? What would he expect when he came home the next day?

Certainly not a physical closeness, she hoped.

No, of course he wouldn't, she thought, turning and surveying the room she'd just prepared for him. He might feel an ambiguous physical affinity for her, but without his memory, she was a virtual stranger to him, and she was certain he wouldn't want to make love to someone he didn't know. It wasn't in his cautious nature. Furthermore, given his injuries, making love was probably the last thing on his mind.

But Aiden would expect *something* from her. Familial warmth. Small signs of affection.

Jill groaned in dread, not because she would find that difficult. Just the opposite. The way Aiden was acting, it would be all too easy to slide into the illusion that they *were* happy, that he still loved her, or, more dangerous, that he'd really changed.

She headed for the adjoining bath to check on the towels. Maybe she should've taken Eric's advice after all and set Aiden up in an apartment with a nurse.

But everything inside her balked at the coldness of that solution. Besides, Dr. Grogan said Aiden's memory would return faster at home, and that was the important thing, wasn't it? To get Aiden well again?

She turned off the bathroom light, crossed the guest room and turned off that light, as well. Then she headed for the stairs and her own ridiculously large king-size bed, the bed she'd shared until recently with Aiden. She was too tired to worry about Aiden's homecoming any longer.

Sufficient to know she was doing the right thing in bringing him home. Besides, it would only be for a couple of weeks. Surely his memory would be back by then, and if it wasn't, Dr. Grogan would see Aiden in his office and make it come back.

In the meantime, she'd just keep reminding herself that the man she was bringing home tomorrow wasn't really Aiden, just an incomplete version of him, and that one day soon the rest of him would inevitably be back.

So, you see, there's really nothing to worry about, she

told herself as she slipped between the cool percale sheets. *Nothing to worry about at all.*

She almost believed it, too.

Aiden was released from the hospital before lunch the next day. At the main entrance he got out of the wheelchair he'd been made to ride in and hitched his crutch under his arm.

"Do you need to get your car, Mrs. Morse?" asked the stout, middle-aged nurse who'd wheeled Aiden.

"No. I'm parked right out front," Jill replied. "I can take over from here."

The nurse turned to her patient, adjusting his jacket over the sling supporting his broken arm. "Do you have your prescription for Percodan?"

"Yes, ma'am," Aiden answered, even though it was Jill who'd pocketed the prescription.

"And the appointment card Dr. Grogan gave you?"

"That, too. I'm supposed to see him at his office in Boston in two weeks."

"Okay, good. In the meantime..."

"I know. Just hang loose."

The nurse smiled. "Not too loose."

"Anything else?" Aiden asked her with a flirtatious grin.

"Yeah. You take good care of yourself, you hear?"

Jill was stunned to see the woman blinking back tears. Even more stunned to see Aiden embrace her.

"I will," he said. "Thanks for everything you've done."

"Aw, go on." The nurse waved him off, then, sniffling delicately, pushed the wheelchair back into the lobby.

Left standing in the entry, Aiden gazed out the glass door. "Well, let's go home." He lifted his chin to a determined angle. "Let's go find out who I am."

Jill walked him to her station wagon and helped him into the front seat. Then she slipped behind the wheel and pulled away from the curb. Her movements were stiff and jerky.

She'd never had Aiden home for more than a couple of days at a time and didn't know how he was going to react. She strongly suspected it wouldn't be with glee. He much preferred being at the office or on the road. Even when he was home, he usually spent his time working in his study.

But without his memory he was no longer able to do that. How on earth would he fill his time? Boredom was bound to set in, followed quickly by a foul mood, she was sure.

Another thing that had Jill on edge was his reaction to Maddy. When he was home, she usually tried to keep the baby away from his study and out of his hair. Quite often she took Maddy for a walk or created errands just to get them out of the house. But how would she do that for two weeks? Three weeks or four? Good Lord, she hoped Aiden wasn't going to remain amnesic and housebound for that long.

Her reluctance to get home and begin the ordeal led her to driving Aiden around Wellington, presumably to reacquaint him with the community where they lived.

"It's a small town, only about eight thousand people," she explained, driving slowly through the older residential neighborhood in which the hospital was located. "There's a map in the glove compartment, if you want to get your bearings."

But Aiden didn't reach for the glove compartment. He was too busy studying the houses and street signs they passed. "Why are we here? Living in Wellington?"

Jill shrugged. "It's one of the more desirable bedroom communities of Boston. Lots of executives live here."

"Do we have friends here?" He'd already learned they had no relatives in the area.

"Friends? Sure." Jill braked at a stop sign.

"Well, maybe a better word is acquaintances." Aiden was too busy for genuine friendships. Quickly she said, "This is the town green. I understand the local militia used to drill here during the Revolution."

Aiden leaned forward, studying the small park, his broad shoulders straining the seat belt.

"We're just coming up to the center of town now. It's quiet. Quaint. Most of the buildings are at least nineteenth century. Many, eighteenth."

Aiden's eyes, she noticed, were luminous with interest.

"You usually have your hair trimmed there." She pointed to the left.

"I have my hair cut at a place called Shear Delight?"

Jill couldn't help laughing at his appalled expression. "Yes. So do I."

He rolled his eyes. "So, how long have we lived here?"

She was about to tell him, then caught herself. "You'll be better off remembering on your own."

He grumbled good-naturedly—he'd been hearing that a lot. "Can we stop for a minute?" he asked.

"Sure." She swerved toward the curb in front of the town's weekly newspaper office.

Aiden sat forward, taking in the street with avid concentration. "It isn't *un*familiar," he said. "Just... murky."

Suddenly he rolled down the window on his side and took a deep, attentive sniff. At the same time his eyes darted to a small restaurant on the corner diagonal to them.

"Have I eaten there?"

"Yes!" Jill tingled with excitement. "We've gone

there lots of times. It's your favorite restaurant. In Wellington, anyway."

Aiden sat back, looking boyishly pleased with himself. He ran his hand over his mouth. "I'm getting hungry. For prime rib."

Jill laughed, easing the car away from the curb. "That's what you usually order."

Before long they'd left the charming business center and were traveling along Holland Road, the long rural lane that would take them home.

"We live in a newly built-up area about three miles south of the center," she explained.

"A development?"

"It's too nice an area to be called that. House lots are an acre, minimum, and they overlook a lake. A pond really. Homes are all custom built, too." Jill glanced at Aiden. His left hand was gripping the upholstered seat so tight his veins bulged.

Yet, when he spoke, his voice was cool and confident. "It's nice out here. Quiet. I like the woods."

No, not cool and confident. Courageous.

Jill's own grip tightened on the steering wheel. She couldn't let herself get emotionally involved with Aiden's plight, not even if the emotion was only sympathy or admiration. Give an inch today, and tomorrow she'd be in over her head. With Aiden, she'd always been too vulnerable.

"This is Taylor Pond Way," she explained, passing through a stone gate, its base abloom with daffodils and grape hyacinth. "It circles the pond."

"Taylor Pond Way," Aiden softly repeated, committing it to memory.

As the first few houses came into view, he whistled through his teeth. "What the *hell* do I do for a living?" His delivery was so dry, Jill couldn't help laughing.

She left the ring road, climbed a short hill and turned

onto the road where their house was located. "White Oak Lane," Aiden read from the street sign. Here, above the lower road, the view of the pond opened out, its sunshot surface glittering like a spill of silver sequins. When Jill slowed and turned in at their driveway, Aiden gasped with exaggerated, yet sincere, astonishment.

"Can we afford this?"

Swallowing a laugh, she said, "Just barely."

Aiden's mouth remained open all the way to the front door. She turned off the engine, but when she reached for the door handle, he held her back.

"Jill, wait." He looked up at the imposing, two-chimney, center-foyer Colonial. "With me not able to work, how are we able to...?"

"You have excellent disability insurance," she assured him. "You're being compensated well."

"Ah." He nodded, but his eyes remained dark and troubled.

"The airline is also negotiating a settlement. Their representative has been in touch with me twice already. The check will probably take a couple of weeks to arrive, but it should be substantial."

His brow went smooth with relief. "Really? Is it enough for me to retire—by any chance?"

Jill could only guess at his anxiety, unable to remember what exactly he did at work. He recalled that he was in a position of authority in a large corporate setting, and he had an idea he was involved with electronics. But that was as detailed as it got. If she were in his shoes, she'd want to retire, too.

She chose to take a light approach, however. "You, retire? That'd be the day. You'd have to be sedated and straight-jacketed to keep you away from work."

She helped him out of the car and up the brick steps of their home. Reaching to open the front door, she added, "Oh, by the way, the baby-sitter's name is..."

"I remember. Mrs. O'Brien. And she has no idea I'm nuts."

Jill giggled. She supposed what Aiden said wasn't all that funny. It was just the way he said it—loose, understated.

She opened the door and set her purse on the foyer table, between the vase of fresh flowers she always kept there and a bowl of potpourri. "Here, let me help you with your jacket." When she had it off, she hung it in the closet and then removed her own coat.

Looking over her shoulder, she noticed Aiden still standing at the door, looking rather like a guest in a strange house.

"Come on," she urged.

Leaning on his crutch, he hobbled forward, giving the long flight of stairs to the second floor a doleful glance. "Are you sure we live in this house and not that ranch I saw down the road?"

"You're the one who chose it," she needled.

"You don't have to sound so happy about it."

She led him into the living room. He stood on the fringe of the Oriental carpet, his gaze roaming, studying. Trying to find himself in its tasteful traditional furnishings?

Just then Jill heard Mrs. O'Brien's lumbering footsteps coming down the hallway from the back of the house. Presently, the matronly baby-sitter appeared in the doorway.

"It's good to have you home, Mr. Morse. You're looking well," she said politely.

Jill felt Aiden's curious gaze zoom from her to the woman and back again. "She calls me 'Mr. Morse'?" he asked out of the side of his mouth. Jill nudged him with her elbow.

"Thank you," he answered the woman.

"What a horrendous ordeal." Mrs. O'Brien compressed her lips and wagged her head.

"It wasn't fun," Aiden agreed. "But looking on the bright side, surviving a train crash makes a great conversation piece. Don't you think?"

Jill chuckled at his slip-of-tongue.

"Did I say train crash?" Aiden tapped his forehead. "Plane crash."

Still smiling, Jill stooped to pick up a basting brush and a flour sifter. "Any trouble with Maddy?" she asked, her mind turning to the little culprit whose favorite activity these days was emptying kitchen drawers and scattering their contents.

"No, none. She's still napping, but I expect she'll be waking soon. The monitor is on the kitchen counter. Would you like me to stay until you have Mr. Morse settled?"

"That's not necessary, unless you want to join us for lunch."

"Oh, no." The elderly woman shook her head. "I'd only stay if I could be of some help."

"You've helped more than I'll ever be able to repay."

"It's been my pleasure. Well, if you're sure you don't need me—" the woman slipped on a gray coat-sweater "—I'll be off."

Jill saw her to the door.

"She seems nice," Aiden said, turning from the fireplace where he was examining the reproduction Renoir over the mantel. "Though a little skittish. Toward me, at least."

Jill shrugged off his astute remark. "Let me go put lunch in the oven before Maddy wakes up."

"Do you mind if I stay here?"

"Well, of course not, Aiden. You don't have to ask my permission." She hurried off to the kitchen and slipped a ready-made lasagna into the oven.

Returning to the living room, Jill found Aiden prowling the drinks cabinet, opening bottles and sniffing their contents.

"I have a strong sense that I don't drink often, but when I do this might be it." He raised a bottle of Irish Mist. "Am I right?"

Jill suspected she reared back at least three feet. "Yes!"

A satisfied smile brightened his face. "It's like hunting for clues. The trouble is, I never know where they'll turn up."

"Would you like to take the grand tour, or just find your way alone?"

"Oh, the tour, by all means."

She took him into the dining room first, aware that he was examining everything he saw—paintings, chairs, bowls of fruit, the Limoges in the china cabinet. He ran his fingers over the long mahogany table, as if tactile contact might help restore elusive memories of meals enjoyed in this room. Not for the first time it struck her as bizarre—unfathomable really—that he was seeing his possessions with a stranger's eye.

"Is anything familiar?"

He nodded, but not with enthusiasm. "Like the town—murky."

Stepping to the bay window, he peered out at Jill's woodland garden. "Oh," he exclaimed softly. "Will you look at that."

Jill gazed out the window, too. The ground under the trees was a carpet of violet blue. "Yes, the scilla are doing great this year," she agreed. "They've spread so fast."

"Scilla," he repeated slowly, as if he were learning to speak a new language. Come to think of it, he probably was. He'd never taken any interest in her gardening before.

Jill had to remind herself to ignore his interest now. It wasn't genuine, and it would pass as soon as the real Aiden returned.

She took him into his study next. "I'm sure you're going to be spending most of your time in this room in the days to come."

"Why would I do that?"

"Because..." *This is where your life at home is, where you can get away from me and Maddy.* "You just like this room best. You get lots of work done here."

"Ah." He nodded, stepping to the window to take in the view. When he noticed the tennis court, he let out an audible gasp.

This astonishment at material things was another side of Aiden that Jill had never seen before. He'd had that court installed with hardly an eye-blink. It puzzled her. But then, her husband was all mystery these days.

Leaving his study, Aiden gave the staircase a protracted look, his eyes narrowing. "Our room..." he murmured, then fell silent again.

Jill's pulse quickened.

"A blue and gray bedspread, soft, puffy. And windows facing the pond." Abruptly his brow relaxed and he chuckled. "There's a Jacuzzi up there, too."

"You're absolutely right, Aiden! In the master bath." Reality soon tempered her enthusiasm, however. "I, um, didn't think you'd be able to get up and down stairs very well, though, so I made up the guest room for you."

He looked slightly disappointed, and she lowered her guilt-ridden eyes. The truth of the matter was, his ability to climb stairs didn't figure high in her list of reasons for having him sleep downstairs.

"It's this way, just down the hall."

She opened a door on a small room that doubled as a sewing room. "I've already brought down some of your clothes."

Aiden hobbled past her, taking in the bed and other furnishings in a quick sweep. "You're right, of course. I can't get up and down stairs."

"You have bruises, too. I might bump them accidentally," she added, leaving unsaid *if we slept together.*

"Thanks, Jill. I appreciate all you're doing for me."

He sounded genuinely grateful—which did nothing to ease Jill's sense of guilt.

"Let me show you the kitchen."

The kitchen spanned nearly thirty feet across the back of the house and included a breakfast nook and a family room with a fireplace. Two sets of French doors opened onto the deck, two more onto a sunroom. Beyond the deck and sunroom stretched the back lawn, several more gardens, and at the far perimeter, on the other side of a stone wall, the woods.

This was Jill's favorite part of the house and where she and the baby spent most of their time.

Aiden made a full circuit of the long, blue-tiled cooking island, stepping around the playpen and over some toys, checking out the cupboards and appliances he passed on either side. He looked truly astounded. "What a great kitchen. Makes me want to cook something."

Jill's eyebrows arched so high, she was sure they'd disappeared into her hair.

Just then from the nursery monitor came the familiar sounds of Maddy's waking and moving about in her crib: the crunch of the mattress, the thump of a foot hitting the rails.

Aiden zeroed in on the sound. "Is that the baby?"

Jill tensed. "Uh-huh." Aiden's pleasant mood had lulled her into thinking his convalescence wasn't going to be as bad as she'd thought. But he hadn't met Maddy yet, the real test.

She wondered if, when he saw his daughter, he'd experience any of the feelings he harbored for her. Would he remember his aversion to having children? His anger and frustration when Jill became pregnant? His dissat isfaction with his marriage after Maddy was born?

"I have to go see to her now, but it shouldn't take long. Will you be all right?"

"Of course."

"You're sure?"

He frowned, studying her. "Will you get going? She sounds like she might start to cry."

After changing Maddy's diaper and putting on her shoes, Jill carried her downstairs. Aiden had stepped out to the deck and was standing at the rail, looking toward the woods. As Jill entered the kitchen with the baby on her arm, her heartbeat took off, thumping like a jack-hammer.

Which was silly, she reminded herself. Aiden had certainly never hurt Maddy physically. Jill couldn't even claim he'd emotionally abused her. He'd never yelled, never scolded, never denigrated.

He'd just never wanted her.

She pressed a kiss to Maddy's sleep-warm cheek. "Whatever happens, I'll always want you," she whispered. Then, taking a deep breath for courage, she gave the glass door a tap.

Aiden turned. Jill was struck by the mixture of trepidation and expectancy in his face, and realized this couldn't be easy for him, either.

Just then Maddy noticed him and chirped, "Da-ee." Ironically *daddy* was one of her first words. She began to bounce in Jill's arms.

Aiden thrust his hand through his hair and blinked several times. Jill wondered what the nervous gestures signified. Had he remembered? She held her breath.

But when Aiden stepped into the kitchen, it wasn't disappointment or anger she found in his expression.

''She's beautiful,'' he said, totally awestruck. ''She's absolutely beautiful.''

Jill spent the day in a state of unrelieved guardedness, expecting Aiden's pleasant mood to turn sour at any minute. It didn't.

After lunch she and the baby went for a drive to fill Aiden's prescription at the pharmacy. Then, upon returning, they spent some time outside. Jill raked winter leaves, while Maddy explored the crocuses and scilla. She'd meant to keep the house quiet for Aiden, but he didn't seem to care about a quiet house. Before long he joined them, saying the day was too nice to stay inside.

The rest of the day got niggled away in ordinary routine. Jill prepared dinner, they ate, she gave Maddy a bath, put her to bed, then cleaned up the kitchen and read the newspaper.

Through it all, the only negative disposition Aiden displayed involved her, Jill, not the baby, and it really wasn't that negative at all. She simply noticed that occasionally he became quiet and pensive, watching her as if something about her puzzled him. She was sure it was just his subconscious whispering to him, and it would only be a matter of time before he remembered he didn't love her and would rather not be married to her.

Thank heaven he tired early that night. She was exhausted herself—from tension, she figured. She escorted Aiden to the guest room, turned back the bed covers and drew the blinds.

When she turned from the window, she found him fumbling one-handedly with his shirt buttons. Dread crawled over her as she realized he was going to need help undressing.

Procrastinating, she watched him a moment longer. His glossy black hair, usually neatly combed, now lay in attractive windblown swirls over his forehead and ears. His complexion, having been kissed by the bright afternoon sun, glowed with vitality and health.

Jill's gaze traveled the long, muscled length of his body, free of its boardroom attire. She rather liked his rugged virility in denim and flannel. Her eyes returned to his face, to his smoky blue eyes, to his beautifully formed mouth made mysterious and sensitive in the soft light cast by the bedside lamp. Her dread deepened.

Not because she didn't want to touch him, but precisely because she did. Her heart might be crushed; her mind might be set on separation. But her senses, ah, her traitorous senses...would they ever listen to anything but Aiden's physical appeal?

He looked up, saw her watching him, and gave her a sheepish shrug.

"Here, let me get that," she said, not meeting his eyes.

"Thanks. In the hospital, the nurses usually helped."

"Yes." Jill unbuttoned his shirt, aware that her own fingers weren't all that efficient. Trying to avoid contact with his hot skin, she slid the shirt over his left shoulder and off that arm. Then, reaching around him, she brought the shirt forward and eased it over his cast.

She'd seen Aiden without his shirt countless times, but tonight she felt she'd never laid eyes on him before. He exercised regularly, and his body was well-toned. Not bulky with muscle, he was handsomely proportioned, solid and strong. Now, as she gazed at his hair-matted chest, she felt a familiar acceleration of her pulse, a familiar stirring in her blood.

Coughing, she glanced toward the dresser. "Would you like to put those on?" She indicated a folded pair of pajamas.

Aiden stared at them, a tiny frown between his eyes. "I don't usually wear pajamas, do I?" As with so many other small habits, he remembered this one correctly, too.

Jill shook her head.

"Then the answer is no. I'll sleep without."

Glancing up at him, she discovered he was fighting back a grin. "What?" she asked in a thin voice.

"My pants. I'd really prefer sleeping with them off."

"Of course." Taking a deep breath, she undid his belt buckle, then, trying not to think about what she was doing, quickly tugged down his jeans. "Sit," she ordered, and when he had, she yanked at each pant leg. He winced and stiffened.

"Sorry." She remembered his bandaged ankle too late.

She was standing at the closet, fumbling to hang his jeans, when he caught her by one shoulder and turned her to face him.

"Jill, stop. Slow down."

She stared at his chest, her breath shallow and rapid. "What's the matter?"

"I don't know. I was about to ask you that."

She thought fast. "Doesn't it bother you to have a stranger undressing you?"

"But you're not a stranger."

"To you I am. Until you get your memory back." Her mouth was so dry her tongue was practically sticking to the roof of her mouth.

He sighed. "If you want to know the truth, yeah, it bothers me." His frown suddenly gave way to a devilish grin. "Not a whole lot, though."

Jill realized his hand was still on her arm. As unobtrusively as possible, she stepped away from his hold.

"But obviously it bothers you," he said, one eyebrow lifting. "Which I find odd. *You* haven't lost your memory. *You* still know we're husband and wife."

She could tell him the truth, that they were a husband

and wife on the verge of separation, two people who'd forfeited their right to physical intimacy. Or she could think fast again.

"I guess I'm experiencing sympathetic self-consciousness." She forced a smile. "I'm feeling uneasy for you, imagining your uneasiness."

"Well, as I said before, there's no reason to." He sat on the bed and, resting his ankle across his knee, pulled off his sock.

"Sorry," Jill mumbled. "I'm acting dumb."

"No, I'm the one who's sorry, Jill. This can't be easy for you." He removed the other sock and patted the bed beside him.

Swallowing her trepidation, she sat.

"I swear I'll make this up to you when I'm better. And I *will* get better. As fast as I can." He covered her tightly interlaced hands with his and gave them a squeeze. "I'm such a lucky man."

She lifted her eyes to his, and her heart melted under the warmth that met her.

"I have so much," he said ardently, each word invested with feeling. "Of all the lives I could've awakened to... It's like waking up on another planet and finding it's where your guardian angel lives."

Jill felt torn up inside. *You don't know what you're saying, Aiden,* she thought. She lifted her hand and placed her fingers over his lips, not quite touching them. "Shh. You've worked hard for what you have. You made your own luck."

She knew she was sidestepping his point, and he seemed about to tell her so, but she didn't give him the opportunity. Reaching for the bottle of painkillers on the nightstand, she said, "Come on now, under the covers with you. If you really want to get better, the best thing you can do for yourself is rest."

With a sigh of resignation, Aiden complied. She was

relieved to be ending the conversation. Even more relieved to have Aiden's body, clad only in a cast and a pair of undershorts, finally out of sight. She handed him a glass of water and he swallowed the pill.

"If you need anything during the night, don't hesitate to give a shout." She placed his crutch within easy reach, then headed for the door.

There she paused. This caring for Aiden was going to be trickier than she thought. For one thing, living under the delusion they were a happily married couple, Aiden was saying and doing things that were bound to humiliate and anger him when his memory returned. She really ought to put the brakes on that sort of behavior now.

Second, there were her feelings to consider. She was getting sucked into the fantasy that this was really Aiden, that he cared. And that was a surefire path to heartbreak.

"Good night, Aiden." Totally perplexed, because she meant every syllable, she added, "It's good to have you home."

CHAPTER FOUR

JILL awoke to a strange silence. She lifted her head off the pillow and gazed about the room. The sunlight filtering through the blinds at the windows seemed too bright. She sat up and pushed her hair out of her eyes, her nerves prickling with apprehension.

Suddenly she realized what was odd about the silence. She bolted from bed and raced across the hall. Sure enough, Maddy's crib was empty. Jill's heart lodged in her throat as her imagination took irrational flight. Where was her daughter? What evil had befallen her?

And then she heard an unexpected sound coming from downstairs, the distant sound of conversation, and, like someone awakening in degrees, she remembered Aiden was home. Listening harder, she recognized his warm baritone notes intermingled with Maddy's squeals. "What on earth?" she whispered, scowling.

She didn't even bother to return to her room for her robe. Her curiosity propelled her straight downstairs to the kitchen. The scene that greeted her put even more questions in her mind.

"Aiden, what are you doing?"

Maddy was perched on his lap at the table in the breakfast nook, the arm that was in a cast encircling her firmly.

"Making a helluva mess, it seems," he answered, laughing as he scraped oatmeal off the baby's plump cheek with a spoon.

Jill came closer, blinking as if that might clear her confusion. "I can see that. But why?"

Aiden dipped the spoon into a jar of strained peaches

and aimed it at Maddy's eager mouth. He'd never fed the baby before, yet he seemed to know what he was doing. Odd. Perhaps he'd watched her more closely than she thought.

"I was up early," he said, as if that explained everything. He'd already showered and dressed himself, too, Jill noticed—sweats with no fastenings at the waist and a loose zip-front top, which he'd left open. Over his sockless feet he'd slipped Italian leather loafers. Quite a fashion statement, she thought with a suppressed smile.

"But your ankle..."

"Feels a lot better. I don't think I want to try those stairs twice in one day, though."

"Once was probably too much."

He lifted one shoulder in a dismissive shrug. "I heard Maddy moving around," he said, spooning up more cereal, "and you were so tired last night I thought I'd let you sleep in."

Jill suddenly became aware of his gaze traveling over her, from her long, uncombed blond hair to her bare feet peeking out from under the hem of her nightgown. Although the heavy silk wasn't see-through, it clung to her in a way that made her feel vulnerable and totally exposed. She quickly took a seat, folding her arms on the table in front of her in an attempt to shield herself from view.

"How on earth did you manage to carry her?"

Aiden ladled another scoop of oatmeal into his daughter's mouth. "Nothing wrong with my left arm," he said, "and the cast on my right does a great job of protecting it."

Jill was dazed and bewildered. She churned with emotions she didn't understand. "Well, you shouldn't have," she said peevishly. "Your ankle could've given out on the stairs. You could've fallen with her."

"I thought of that. That's why I came down on my

rump." He grinned, too engaging for words. "She seemed to get a real kick out of it, too."

Maddy looked up at him and blessed him with one of her cherubic smiles. "Daddy was goofy, wasn't he?" Aiden said, nuzzling the baby's cheek and tickling her with loud kisses. Maddy squealed and wiggled.

Jill gaped at the two of them, struggling with the image they made. How many times in the past had she dreamed of seeing them interacting like this? How often had she longed for Aiden to wake up to the treasure he had in his daughter? Why was it happening now, when it was too late?

"I still wish you'd called me," she said, vexed. "And please don't do it again. She's a handful now that she's begun to walk. You don't realize how active she is. And how fast."

Aiden stared at her. "Sure I do."

"No, you don't," she insisted more adamantly than she should have.

The morning sunlight pouring over Aiden's face accentuated the frown that slipped into his eyes. It was the same frown she'd occasionally glimpsed yesterday—pensive, puzzled, as if he was trying to figure her out.

"Have you had breakfast yourself?" she asked briskly.

"Not yet."

"Well, Maddy looks to be about done with hers. I'll take her off your hands."

"That's okay. I'm fine."

"No, really, I should," Jill said, getting up and attempting to lift Maddy off his lap. His hold seemed to tighten. The thought occurred to her that they were using the baby in a sort of tug-of-war. "I have to get her dressed for the day. And her diaper, you weren't able to change it, were you?"

Aiden grimaced and shook his head.

"Well, then."

His hold slackened.

Jill carried Maddy upstairs, trying not to think about the disappointment she'd glimpsed in Aiden's eyes when she took the baby from him. Instead, she focused on the harm he could've done if he'd stumbled on the stairs and dropped her. The harm that could've befallen Maddy downstairs, too, if he'd let her get into the wrong cupboard or climb where she shouldn't. He didn't know those things.

As she changed Maddy out of her oatmeal-soggy sleeper, she reluctantly admitted there was more to her reaction than just fear of the physical harm that might've come to her daughter in Aiden's care. She was also mad. Ripping, in fact.

Aiden had no right to be acting the thoughtful husband and doting father—showing her how good life *could* be within their family. It wasn't fair.

This behavior wasn't really his. She had no idea where it was coming from, or why, but she did know it would eventually pass. Knowing that, she felt she was being unfairly teased. Cheated even.

But at least she was capable of understanding. What about Maddy? What would happen if she got attached to her father during this abnormal interlude? What would happen when his memory returned and their lives got back on course? Where would she be when he left and never paid attention to her again? Jill didn't want to see her get hurt. Although Maddy was young and resilient, if Aiden continued to play out the role of father, she'd still miss him and be confused when he dropped out of her life.

Jill dressed Maddy in a soft-knit, two-piece outfit in a shade of pink that accentuated her big blue eyes and fair hair. Standing her on the changing table, Jill gave her an impetuous hug, feeling an upsurge of maternal protectiveness.

This baby might've been a mistake, an "oops" in the birth control game, but she was a mistake Jill would be thankful for the rest of her days. Her life revolved around this little person now, on raising her well, making her feel secure and loved, and giving her a strong sense of self-esteem.

In the past, Aiden hadn't contributed a single thing to their daughter's well-being. As far as Jill could see, this new attention wasn't going to do anything, either. It might even hurt. Jill knew he was sick and needed attention, but he wasn't her first priority. Taking care of her child far outstripped that obligation. And if taking care of Maddy meant protecting her from Aiden, well, so be it. Aiden would just have to cope.

When Jill left the house, Aiden was in his study, examining the bookshelves. "Looking for clues," he quipped. She strapped Maddy into her car seat and together they spent most of the morning running errands. While Aiden had been in the hospital, she'd let a lot of things slide—trips to the cleaners, the bank, the post office, certain stores.

Fortunately Maddy didn't mind gallivanting about town, and she actually liked riding in shopping carts. She especially liked charming shoppers and cashiers with her smiles and ready chirps of "hi." *Hi* was one of her favorite words, probably because she could say it so well, or maybe because people responded with "hi" in return.

Jill's last stop, the garden center, was admittedly self-indulgent, a treat for getting her other chores done. By then, however, the morning was waning and so was Maddy. She began to fuss and rub her eyes. Jill quickly chose a flat of pansies and headed for the check-out.

She arrived home in a better frame of mind. Her anger at Aiden had dulled significantly, reverting to a simple, rational resolve to keep her emotional distance.

She was coming through the kitchen door, Maddy in one arm, shopping bags in the other, just as the telephone began to ring. "I've got it," she called out, not sure where Aiden was.

It was Eric, calling to ask if Brady could stay with her that afternoon. It was a half day of school.

"Sorry it's such short notice, Jill. If you already have plans, I can cancel my afternoon appointments."

But she assured him she was in for the day and would be glad to watch his son.

By the time she hung up, Maddy was clinging to her and whining. Her eyes were heavy with tiredness.

"Somebody's sure ready for a nap," Jill crooned, holding her daughter on one hip, while a bottle of milk warmed in the microwave.

Heading for the stairs, Jill glanced into Aiden's study. He was still there, right where he'd been when she'd left the house.

He was sitting at his computer, the glow from the screen casting an eerie light over his handsome face and disheveled hair. He seemed absorbed, and not necessarily happy. In spite of her earlier anger at him, she was impressed by how hard he was working to piece together his life and become whole again.

Ironically, he thought he was a burden to her in his present condition and that in getting well he'd be doing her and their marriage a favor. Jill felt a pang of guilt for not telling him the truth of the matter, that the closer he got to being himself, the closer he'd bring them to splitting. But maybe it was better he didn't realize that.

"Hey, Jill." He looked up from his computer and his expression softened. She told herself to ignore his response; this wasn't really Aiden.

"Hi, little stuff," he said to Maddy.

"Hi." Tired as she was, Maddy lifted her head off Jill's shoulder and gave Aiden a smile.

"I'm going to put her down for her nap."

"Okay. Good. Come back when you're done. I can't wait to tell you what happened while you were gone."

Jill tensed. Had he remembered something? "I'll be down soon."

As soon as the baby was asleep, Jill joined Aiden in his study. "What happened?"

Aiden pushed away from the screen and swiveled toward her. She braced herself, waiting for him to tell her his memory had returned. "This." He waved at the computer. "I know my way around it."

"Oh," she said, inexplicably relieved. And then, "Oh!" The significance of finding him working at his computer hadn't occurred to her. She was so used to seeing him here.

"It was the damnedest thing. I took off the dust cover, pressed the on switch, and the sound of the power surging through was immediately familiar and reassuring. Before I'd thought about it, I'd pressed some keys and started a program."

Jill sat on the edge of his desk. "That's weird."

"Isn't it?"

She glanced at the obligatory photograph of her that Aiden kept on his desk. It had been moved closer to the computer screen. She tried not to think about the significance of that.

"Dr. Grogan mentioned that sensory experiences would be a good catalyst for triggering memory," he added, sitting back in a relaxed fashion and rocking the chair, "and I'd be willing to bet that's what happened here. The sound of the computer starting up jogged my memory."

"Could be. But maybe your computer skills were accessible right along."

"Maybe. In any case, I was thinking, if I went to my office I might remember even more."

"At ABX?"

"Yes."

"Hmm. That could be tricky. You don't remember your co-workers."

"I was hoping you'd go with me and fend them off."

Jill chuckled at the image. "Why don't we go after hours, when there are fewer people there. Better yet, how about Sunday, when nobody's there?"

"I can do that?"

"Sure. You have a key, and the watchmen know you."

"Great. Let's do it." Aiden's smiling eyes held hers steadily. It was one of those looks that started out communicating pleasure in the plan they'd just made, then gradually shifted and intensified, becoming so much more. As the moment spun out, his look reached deeper and deeper, and the air between them heated up with awareness.

Finally, almost unable to breathe, Jill glanced aside at the screen. "So, um, did you find anything useful in your computer?"

"Uh...yeah." He shifted his position. "Lots of stuff. For instance, I called up a file titled 'Calendar' and found my daily schedule. Lists of appointments. Business lunches. Trips to other cities." His glance slid back to Jill. "Lots of trips. Seems I'm a busy guy."

Jill blinked and looked away, saying nothing.

"Apparently, this calendar contains only work-related activities, though, because I didn't find anything to do with my personal life—although, to be honest, I can't imagine how anyone could fit a personal life into the itinerary I just read." He chuckled. "I do have one, don't I?"

He was smiling, but Jill could see questions in his eyes, the beginnings of doubts behind his jocularity. Had he gotten a glimpse of himself and not understood what he saw? Had he not liked it?

Evasively she replied, "You're a man with a lot of responsibilities."

"I guess." Frowning at the screen, he planted his elbow on the arm of his chair and his chin in his hand.

"Did you find anything else?"

He shook off his preoccupation. "Sure. Lots of business correspondence. Nothing made sense or rang any bells, though. Seems I remember my computer skills, but not dealings with people."

Growling in mild frustration, he rose from his chair. "Want to have some lunch while the baby's asleep? Just you and me?" He waggled his eyebrows in a comic leer.

"That'd be different." Jill didn't mean anything by her comment, except that the baby left her little time these days for personal pursuits, but he glanced at her sharply. Was he beginning to suspect something was wrong between them?

"Any calls while I was gone?" she asked quickly. Aiden turned off the overhead light, and they started down the hall to the kitchen.

"Yes. That was the other thing I wanted to tell you. Someone named Greg Simmons called from ABX."

"Greg Simmons?" Jill stopped in her tracks.

"Mmm. You know the name?"

"Oh, Aiden. He's your boss. He's *everybody's* boss. He's the president and CEO of the company."

Aiden grimaced comically, and she had to remind herself to keep her emotional distance.

"What did you say to him?"

"Nothing incriminating...I think. Fortunately he

didn't ask me anything about work. I was worried he would. He just wanted to know how I was feeling. I told him I was in a lot of discomfort and on heavy-duty pain-killers. I figured that would excuse any dumb stuff I said.''

Suppressing another smile, she said, ''You should've let the answering machine take it.''

''In the future I will, believe me. His call reminded me how important it is for me to get better. That's why I want to go into the office, see if I can hurry this up.''

He slid into a chair in the breakfast nook, eyeing the shopping bag on the table. ''What did you buy?''

''Oh, just stuff.'' She began to empty the bag. Aspirins. Wrapping paper. Band-Aids. Diaper cream.

''Oh, I see you had some pictures developed, too.'' Aiden looked at her hopefully. ''May I?''

She shifted uncomfortably. ''They're...just of Maddy's birthday.''

The gleam of anticipation in his eyes deepened. Reluctantly she slid the envelope across the table. He opened it and took out the photographs. While he was looking through them, Jill busied herself with putting the other items away. But she wasn't so busy that she didn't notice his look of expectancy draining away.

''I'm not in any of the pictures.''

''You...weren't here.''

''How come?''

Jill felt old hurts rising, churning up her anger. She opened a cupboard, took out a can of tuna, and tried to keep from blurting, *Because you don't give a damn about your daughter.*

She said, ''You were away on business.''

''Oh.'' He shuffled through the pictures again. ''I'm ashamed to say this, but when exactly was her birthday?''

Yes, you should be ashamed. ''A week ago Tuesday.''

She opened the can of tuna, drained the water from it and began to make two sandwiches at the cooking island.

"I was in Detroit," Aiden said unexpectedly.

Jill looked up, startled.

"No, I don't remember. I just got a mental image of my calendar."

"Oh."

He held up a photograph. "Who are all these people?"

"Friends," she answered vaguely.

"But who? What are their names? How are we connected?"

Jill didn't want to think about Maddy's birthday. It reminded her of everything wrong with their marriage. "You know Dr. Grogan said you should remember those things on your own."

She placed the sandwiches on the table, brought over two glasses and a container of apple juice, and sat down. Her shoulders were stiff and her neck muscles ached.

Aiden, she noticed, was watching her again, those clever blue eyes too sharp and thorough. All at once his perplexity cleared. "Ah, now I get it."

"Get what?" She poured juice into his glass.

"Why you're mad at me."

She knew her color was deepening. "I'm not mad at you."

"No? Something's sure been bugging you, and I think I finally figured out what. I missed Maddy's birthday. Her *first* birthday."

"It was unavoidable." She stared out the window, too miffed to look at him.

"Was it?"

"Yes. Forget it."

"How can I? I feel terrible."

"We survived." Apparently her bitterness came through, despite her effort to hide it.

"Boy, you know how to hang on to a grudge." He lifted his sandwich clumsily with his left hand. Some of the filling fell out. "Well, for all it's worth now, I'm sorry I wasn't here."

Sorry doesn't cut it, she thought, taking an unappetizing bite of her sandwich. Apparently, she was still scowling.

"Jeez, Jill, give me a break. I'm the one who wasn't here. I'm the one who lost out. My daughter's first birthday is never going to come again."

She tried to ease up. "Sorry. I'm really okay with this. Can we move on?"

"Fine by me. That's what I'm *trying* to do."

Just then Jill thought she heard the grinding gears of the school bus as it came up the hill. She tilted her head, her eyes growing alert. "Yep, that's the school bus, all right." She got to her feet.

Talking around another bite of sandwich, Aiden asked, "Do we have another child you haven't told me about?"

"Yes. His name's Brady." Smiling, she added, "He's a neighbor. I sometimes mind him after school until his father comes home from work. Today's a half day though. He'll be with us all afternoon."

Before Aiden could object or ask questions, she hurried off to the front door to greet the little boy.

As soon as Aiden saw Brady, Jill knew he recognized him as one of the children who'd attended Maddy's birthday party. Jill wondered if he was curious about the man who appeared with Brady in so many of the birthday pictures. She caught him looking through the photographs several more times before he finished lunch, lingering over those where Eric appeared. An uneasy feeling grew inside her.

After lunch Aiden retired to the guest room, where he elevated his ankle and wrapped it in ice. It was healing nicely, but he was doing all he could to hurry the process. Jill assembled the ingredients for chocolate chip cookies, tied an apron around Brady, and for the next hour tried to put her husband out of her mind.

"Hi." Jill stepped back from the front door to let Eric into the foyer. A gust of cold, damp air came with him. Typically, April was proving itself a chancy month, one day balmy, the next sliding back toward winter.

"We heard you pull up. Brady's just putting on his jacket." Jill turned and smiled at the six-year-old who was struggling to fasten a stubborn zipper. Maddy was trying to help.

"Come here, Tiger," Eric said, pushing back his trench coat and squatting down. His son approached, preoccupied by the zipper, his tongue clamped between his teeth. Eric gave Jill a grin that communicated his delight in his son. Picking up her daughter, she gave him a smile in return.

"Have you had fun with Jill and Maddy today?"

"Uh-huh." Brady finally zipped up his windbreaker and gave his father his full attention. "We made chocolate chip cookies."

"Oh, wow. What a lucky guy. I wish I had some..."

"Here." Jill picked up a plastic container full of cookies from the foyer table. "Now you can spare me the heavy hints."

Getting to his feet, Eric took the container and smiled. "Thanks." Then, leaning closer, he asked under his breath, "How's it going—you know, with Aiden home?" Sympathy poured from his warm hazel eyes.

"Not bad. I'm hanging in."

"Is he giving you any trouble?"

"No." She put Maddy down and watched her toddle

toward her toy xylophone which was under the coffee table in the living room.

"Are you sure?" Eric persisted.

Jill became somewhat annoyed. Did Eric *want* Aiden to be giving her trouble? "I'm positive."

"Well, if you need any help..."

Jill noticed Eric's eyes suddenly fix on a point behind her. She turned to find Aiden watching them from the doorway of his study, a hawkish intentness in his expression. She stepped away from Eric, realizing quite suddenly how close they were standing.

"Hi, there, Aiden." Eric lifted a hand in greeting. "Good to see you home. How are you feeling?" Being a real-estate salesman, affability came easily to him, even when he didn't mean it.

Aiden propped his crutch under his arm and came forward. He wasn't smiling, Jill noticed. "I'm doing very well, thanks," he said.

"Good, good. That was a hell of an experience."

"Not one I want to repeat anytime soon."

Jill wondered why Aiden had come out of his study. After that phone call from Mr. Simmons, the logical thing would be to avoid running the risk of tripping up in conversation with anyone else.

Eric asked, "How long before you can get back to work?"

Jill emitted a tiny squeak of surprise as Aiden slipped his hand around her waist.

"I'm not sure. I'm in no hurry, though." His fingers tightened, pulling her closer.

Eric's gaze moved from Aiden's hand to Jill's eyes. His mouth hardened even as he said, "Is there anything I can do for you while I'm here?"

What did he *want* to do? she wondered. Lift some heavy furniture? Take Aiden outside and challenge him to a duel?

"No, we're fine," Aiden said. His hand slid upward from her waist over her ribs and down again. "But thanks for asking." Ah, the undercurrents flowing through this prosaic conversation.

Eric sighed. "Okay. Well, I'll be taking Brady home, then. Thanks again for watching him." He opened the door. "And for the cookies."

"Divorced, right?" Aiden asked as soon as Eric had driven away.

"Yes." Jill stepped away from her husband's possessive hold.

"Great. That's just great," he muttered.

"What are you talking about?"

"I don't know," he railed in frustration, throwing up his arms, even the one in the cast. "I don't know, and that's the damnable part of it."

"Aiden, if you're thinking what I think you're thinking..." Jill laughed nervously. Surely he didn't remember the wild accusation he'd made the morning of the plane accident. "Let me assure you there's nothing going on between me and Eric."

Aiden looked at her, his gaze hard and direct. "Maybe you don't think so..."

"Neither does Eric. He's just a friend."

"How good a friend, Jill?"

She knew she was turning red and hated herself for letting it happen. "This is a silly conversation. I've got better things to do." With that, she pushed past Aiden and headed for the kitchen.

That night after Maddy was asleep and Aiden had settled in the guest room, Jill quietly slipped out to the sun porch with a glass of Chablis and curled up in one of the newly cushioned wicker chairs she'd found at a flea market last summer.

At dinner she'd apologized to Aiden for that remark about their conversation being silly. But she hadn't recanted. There really wasn't anything going on between her and Eric.

As she sat there, remembering Aiden's accusations, an unbidden smile softened her lips. As contradictory as her reaction was, she'd liked the feel of Aiden's hand at her waist. She'd enjoyed his jealousy.

The Aiden she knew wasn't in the habit of displaying such emotions. He was too reserved, too intent on protecting whatever was going on inside him, too afraid that opening himself up to her would betray some dangerous vulnerability. She hadn't realized he was even capable of anything like jealousy.

Where was that coming from? she wondered. And more importantly, why was she getting caught up in it? Her smile faded.

She couldn't let that happen. She had to continue to resist this new, charming Aiden. She had to remember he wasn't going to last. Today his computer skills had returned. Who knew what tomorrow would bring?

She took a sip of wine and laid her head back against the cool chintz cushion. It was a fine line she was walking, this taking care of Aiden. He needed her attention and she'd gladly give it, but she couldn't get too involved. She had to remember to keep her heart out of the giving.

A fine, difficult line, but she believed she could do it. All she had to do was recall an incident from the past year, any incident—going through labor alone, for instance, or his telling her he wished it didn't exist, meaning the baby growing inside her—and her resolve returned revitalized.

But if bitter recollections didn't work, she could always look to the future. Did she want to continue living the lonely existence of a business widow? Did she want her daughter growing up ignored, thinking there was something wrong with her, something inherently unlovable?

Jill finished her wine and got to her feet. She was positive she could get through Aiden's ordeal without getting emotionally involved. For Maddy, she'd find the strength to face anything.

Jill was dredging a load of laundry out of the washer the next day when she heard a noise that sounded suspiciously like her car starting. She stepped out of the laundry and opened the garage door. Sure enough, Aiden was sitting behind the wheel, grinning at her through the windshield.

She planted her hands on her hips, tilted her head and raised her eyebrows. He read her body language and laughed.

Sticking his head out the window, he said, "It's just occurred to me that your car's an automatic."

"So? You have a cast on your arm."

"So?"

"Aiden!"

"Aiden," he mimicked. "Need anything from town?" His smile was waggish.

"No, I don't," she said firmly. "What I need is for you to..." But before she could say another word, he lifted his cast and waggled the tips of his fingers at her. Then, looking in the rearview mirror, he backed the car out of the garage.

Jill stared at the retreating vehicle in a stupor. She wasn't really worried about him getting into an accident. Aiden was an excellent driver. Even one-handed, he was probably better than most. What worried her was his getting lost.

She'd taken him around town after his release from the hospital, but she wasn't sure that was enough for him to remember his way. And what if he met up with someone he should know?

She gave his sports car a glance and thought about following. But Maddy was napping.

Should she wake her? Bundle her into the car and take off in pursuit? No, of course not. Should she call the police?

"Augh! Aiden Morse," she cried aloud, "you're driving me crazy!"

Jill was folding the freshly dried laundry when she heard her station wagon pull into the garage again. She heaved a sigh of relief. At the same moment, Maddy awakened from her nap and gave out a wail. Jill turned off the monitor and ran upstairs.

"Hey, pun'kin," she sang, entering the nursery. "Did you have a nice nap?"

Standing in the crib, Maddy raised her arms, asking to be picked up, and said something that sounded close enough to mom-mom-mom to reduce Jill to putty.

"Oh, you are so smart," she said lifting Maddy from her crib and wrapping her close. She loved how the baby felt upon waking, all warm and cuddly.

Jill changed Maddy's diaper and outfit, which had also gotten wet during her nap, then carried her and a favorite stuffed bear downstairs to the kitchen. "Are you hungry, sweetie? Are you ready for your lu—" The words died on her lips when she noticed the kitchen table. "What on earth...?"

On the table in front of Maddy's high chair sat a yellow-and-white birthday cake decorated in a Winnie-the-Pooh motif. It was flanked by three colorfully wrapped packages, two mylar balloons—and one nervously grinning father.

CHAPTER FIVE

"HAPPY Birthday, Madison Kay," Aiden said, coming forward and placing a kiss on his daughter's cheek. As he did so, his arm pressed into Jill, making her keenly aware of him in a physical way. Whether he was aware of her or not, she didn't know, but he certainly took his time stepping back.

"I'm sorry I couldn't be here for your birthday," he continued, fingering one of Maddy's silky blond ringlets. "I'm hoping I can make it up to you today and you won't hold it against me."

Although he kept his eyes on Maddy, Jill sensed he was really talking to her. She wanted to say something, but suddenly her throat felt too tight for words.

To cover her unexpected sentimentality, she made herself busy, seating Maddy in her high chair.

"Is this okay with you?" Aiden asked.

Jill slid the white plastic tray onto the chair and, keeping her tone neutral, said, "Yes, sure. Maddy ought to have her lunch first, though. Before cake."

"Oh, of course. I meant our having a belated celebration."

Jill wanted to be angry. She wanted to tell him no, it was too late, and his missing the party was only a symptom of the problem, anyway. She wanted him to know she was irrevocably fed up and permanently hurt.

But the man looking back at her wouldn't understand. The man looking back at her only wanted to make amends. Because the man looking at her wasn't really Aiden.

"It's lovely, Aiden," she conceded, meaning every syllable. "Perfectly lovely."

As soon as they'd finished with their lunch, Aiden lit the solitary candle on Maddy's cake, and he and Jill sang "Happy Birthday." Maddy played up to the attention with an array of delightful squeaks and giggles. She even clapped her hands when they did.

"Okay, kid, have fun." Aiden placed a large piece of chocolate cake with ice cream on the high chair tray. Jill grimaced as Maddy sank her chubby fingers into the goo.

"Oh, wait! I want a picture of this." Aiden hurried to the sideboard where Jill kept her camera. With Maddy growing so quickly, she always kept it loaded with film.

"Here." He handed Jill the camera. "Get a shot of the two of us together." He strode to the high chair and squatted down beside it. "I want her to have proof I was here."

Jill aimed and snapped, then said, "Let me take another for good measure."

Aiden moved a little closer to his daughter so that his head was almost touching hers. Through the viewfinder, Jill saw it was going to be a great picture: Aiden's coarse black hair juxtaposed to his daughter's angel-fine blond; the contrasts everywhere of hard and soft, strong and delicate; the disarming similarities in the shape of eyes and nose and chin.

Just as Jill was about to press the shutter button, however, Maddy picked up her plate and turned to look at her father, inadvertently hitting him square in the face.

Snap!

Jill lowered the camera and gazed at Aiden, thunderstruck. He was still sitting on his heels, motionless, with glops of chocolate cake and vanilla ice cream all over his face. A series of emotions paraded through her. Tension. Was he about to explode? Sympathy. He was such a mess! And finally amusement.

"Oh, sweetheart, what did you do to Daddy?" Jill bit her lip hard but began to laugh, anyway. A dollop of ice cream slid off Aiden's eyebrow. He caught some of it on his tongue.

One of the expressions Maddy had learned to say, when something broke or spilled, was *uh-oh.* "Uh-oh," she said now. Aiden's lips twitched and his shoulders began to shake.

"Hold it," Jill instructed and snapped another picture. Then, still fighting back laughter, she hurried to the sink and wet a towel to clean up the mess.

After the mop-up was done and they'd consumed their cake in a more civilized manner, Aiden helped Maddy open her presents. Jill sat close at hand, bemused, wondering what he'd bought. What *would* a man choose for a one-year-old daughter he didn't know or remember?

The first gift was a yellow school bus with three roly-poly play people inside. They could be removed by a back door or through the top of the bus. Jill knew instantly that Maddy would love it. And she did.

"Brrrm, brrrm!" She rolled the bus across her tray with vigorous arm movements, adding sound effects. She was so taken with the bus that she paid no attention when Aiden held up the next gift.

Shrugging, he said, "You open it," and handed it to Jill.

Jill tore off the paper. "Look, honey. You've got another present," she said, lifting the lid of the box. "Isn't it..." Her eyes widened and she choked on a laugh. "A baseball glove?"

Maddy looked up, but the leather glove held no interest for her. However, the big pink bow from the box did. She grabbed it and scrunched it into her new bus along with the three roly-polies. "Brrrm!"

"Yes, a baseball glove." Aiden refused to look anything but righteous. "These days girls have to know how to throw and catch every bit as much as boys do."

"Sure. But maybe you could've waited a few months?"

He angled a sorrowful look her way. "Mothers take the fun out of everything."

The last box was large and bore the glossy gold logo of one of the better department stores in the area. When Jill lifted the cover and turned back the tissue paper, she melted. Aiden had bought Maddy an outfit. She'd never known him to be interested in buying clothing before, for anyone, and the image of him roaming the children's department, searching through racks of dainty apparel, did strange things to her.

She lifted the outfit, a navy and white sailor dress that would be perfect for the hot summer days ahead. And then she noticed the other garment, a nearly identical ensemble in *her* size. "Oh!" she cried softly, too surprised for words.

"It's a mother-daughter set," Aiden explained. "If you don't like it, it can be exchanged. I just thought...well..." His gaze traveled over her appreciatively. She got the feeling he was visualizing her in it. "I thought the two of you would look cute dressed alike. But if you think it's too cute..."

"No. I do like it, Aiden. I'm just a little overwhelmed. It's Maddy's birthday, not mine."

He breathed out a laugh. "Well, see, that's the thing. Since I don't know when your birthday is, I figured I'd cover all my bases today."

"Thank you." Jill sat back with the outfit in her arms and tears in her eyes. She gazed at her baby, still playing with her bus; gazed at her husband, who was gazing back. And suddenly she realized she was in deep trouble. Her resistance was melting like a sheet of thin ice. It was impossible to remain detached when dealing with a man like Aiden, impossible to pretend he wasn't getting to her. And the worst part was, she didn't even know what she wanted to do about it anymore.

Dr. Grogan phoned later that afternoon, wanting to know how Aiden was doing.

"Pretty well." Holding the receiver in the crook of her neck, Jill pulled off her gardening gloves and dropped them on the potting bench in the sunroom. "He's upstairs soaking in a whirlpool at the moment."

"Good. That should ease his aches and pains somewhat."

"That's what we're hoping."

"Are there any significant changes in his condition?"

"Physically, he's coming along fine." She stepped over the blocks Maddy was playing with on the warm sisal-covered floor, and took a seat in her favorite wicker chair. "His bruises are fading, he's stopped taking the painkillers you prescribed, and today he's walking without his crutch. Mentally, though, his progress hasn't been anything to write home about."

"Well, it's only been a week since the accident."

Was it only that? Jill had lost all sense of time.

"He's remembered small things," she offered. "He's also been playing with his computer. He remembers his way around programs and files."

"Oh, that's something."

"Mmm. He wants to go into work to see if something there might jog his memory. We're going in on Sunday night when nobody'll be in the building."

"No harm in that," the psychiatrist said agreeably. "How's his temperament?"

"Surprisingly good." Jill smiled softly, remembering their birthday celebration earlier.

"He's not showing signs of impatience or frustration with his condition?"

Jill bent forward and began building a tower of blocks. "Nothing I can't live with."

"No withdrawal or despondency?"

"Uh-uh." After a few seconds of reflection, "I know. You'd think a person in his situation *would* be frustrated or despondent, but he isn't."

"Well, I can't say that I'm all that surprised. Your husband's a remarkable man, Jill. Did you know that after the plane landed he stayed onboard helping the flight attendants get other people off?"

Sitting back, Jill went quietly still. "No, I didn't know that. I remember he was one of the last passengers to leave the plane. How did you come by this bit of news?"

"I've been interviewing some of the crew, trying to get a fuller picture of what happened. I think Aiden may be awarded a commendation of some sort."

"Really?" She frowned. "But how did he manage? He was injured himself. He had a broken arm!"

"Amazing, isn't it, the power the mind has over the body?"

Jill leaned on the arm of the chair, gripping her head in her hand. If she'd been confused before, now she was totally at sea.

"In any case," the doctor said, "let me know if his disposition changes—if it becomes too much for you to handle."

"I will."

"We have an appointment in a week, but I can always fit you in if something unexpected arises." It seemed the doctor was getting ready to close.

"Dr. Grogan, do you mind if I ask a stupid question?"

"You know the saying—the only questions that are stupid are the ones that go unasked."

"Is it possible for a person's basic personality to change during an interlude of amnesia?"

In the subsequent silence, she entertained an image of the psychiatrist stroking his beard. "Off the cuff, I'd say no. Why? Is Aiden behaving in a significantly different manner?"

Jill twisted the phone cord around her hand. "Well...yes." Staying onboard a downed plane to help others get off didn't sound like the self-serving Aiden she knew, but she refrained from mentioning that, preferring to cite a less negative example. "Among other things, he's more relaxed around our daughter, more willing to spend time with her. In fact, he seems to actually enjoy being with her."

"And he never used to?"

"No. That was one of the reasons our marriage was in trouble."

"I'm reluctant to put an interpretation on his behavior over the phone—you know, without talking to him—but it could be he's just more relaxed in general, now that he doesn't have to go in to work."

Jill weighed the merits of that possibility and found it came up lacking. "That would be assuming he'd wanted to be with our daughter all along."

"You don't think he did?"

"I know he didn't. When we got married, it was never his intention to have a child. And another thing, he used to like going to work. Loved it. Staying home is what made him crazy."

The line hummed with silence for an uncomfortably long while. "Well, as I said, I doubt his disorder has changed his basic personality."

"It's done something to it," Jill insisted.

"I'll certainly address the issue when he comes in to see me."

Jill slumped with disappointment. Apparently, the

doctor wasn't going to hazard a guess as to what was happening.

But then, without talking to Aiden, how could he? Would she trust him if he did?

"I didn't mean to put you on the spot. It's just something I've been curious about."

"No problem, Jill. Is there anything else I can help with?"

She gulped. Yes, there was one other thing. It was the fact that Aiden assumed they were still contentedly married. Or, more to the point, that she'd been picking up indications he was still physically attracted to her and thinking of doing something about it.

But suddenly she was reluctant to enter the subject into their conversation. What was the point? She'd already put Aiden in a separate bedroom, thereby eliminating the risk of contact at night. And, to be honest, she might be wrong about his intentions. He hadn't actually done anything except give her a few evocative looks.

Besides, if Aiden did do something, she hardly needed Dr. Grogan's advice in order to handle it. She'd simply put Aiden off with excuses. There were any number she could draw on, and if he rejected her excuses, there was always the truth. It was a last resort, but she'd tell him they were splitting. There would be no arguing with that.

"No. That's about all for now, Doctor. Thank you."

Jill hung up the phone, wishing she felt more at ease.

Leaving Maddy in the care of the ever-dependable Mrs. O'Brien, Jill drove Aiden to ABX Industries the next evening. The plant, which housed both executive offices and a manufacturing division, was located in an industrial park just outside Boston. The grounds were Sunday-quiet and empty, except for the handful of cars belonging to the watchmen.

She pulled into the parking slot with Aiden's name on it, aware that he was studying the sprawling, four-story, yellow brick building with quiet but intense interest. How daunting it must be to face the place where one worked and not remember a thing about it.

Jill reached across the front seat and gave Aiden's arm a squeeze for reassurance and courage. "Shall we go in?"

He nodded and opened the door on his side.

A uniformed security guard met them at the entrance.

"Hello," Jill said, smiling at the young man.

"Mrs. Morse." He dipped his head in greeting. "How are you feeling, Mr. Morse?"

"I can't complain." Aiden had brought along his crutch to give the impression he was worse off than he really was. "Do you mind if my wife and I spend some time in my office? My work—there's some catching up I need to do."

The young man frowned, his head tilting in curiosity. "Sure. Just let me turn off the alarm on that wing."

Walking through the lobby, Aiden whispered, "What did I do wrong?"

"You're not the sort of person who usually asks permission."

"Oh."

Jill knew the building well. She'd worked here right out of college, in the "sales pit." That was what everyone called the area where the entry-level salespeople worked. She was never quite sure if the name referred to the nature of the job—as in, it was the pits—or to the architectural configuration of the area.

The ceiling was two stories high, the only natural light coming through a glass-domed roof above. A midfloor mezzanine ran along three walls, and off that mezzanine lay the executive offices. Looking up from her desk, Jill had found it easy to imagine herself in a pit, especially when someone was leaning on the balcony railing, looking down.

Jill stepped out of the elevator onto the executive floor and crossed to that railing now, giving her old workstation a glance. Even more cubicles had been jammed into the space below.

"Anything wrong?" Aiden inquired, coming up behind her.

"Uh, no." She smiled over her shoulder. "Come on. Your office is down this way."

"You've visited me at work before—obviously."

Jill only nodded. He still didn't remember how they'd met and she hadn't told him. It was one of those things she felt he'd be better off remembering on his own. Besides, she found it uncomfortable reliving those days when she was so naively happy.

She watched him insert his key in the lock of his office door. He'd chosen the correct key instinctively. It wasn't till they had passed through his secretary's office, however, that it dawned on him. He glanced backward as if the lock had just nipped at his heels. "Well, I'll be!"

"Well, I'll be, is right." Jill chuckled.

But it soon became apparent that was all the progress he'd made. He stood on the thick burgundy carpeting of his office, his roving gaze soaking up the details...and recognizing nothing. "Whoever Aiden Morse is, he sure likes nice things." He whistled, shaking his head. "Original works of art, even at the office."

Jill could've told him he believed that surrounding himself with the right props was vital. When aiming for the summit, he'd often said, one had to act as if one belonged at the summit. Sometimes she wondered if she wasn't a prop herself.

She knew she was considered a good-looking woman, an assessment she accepted without any vanity because she'd grown up a gawky girl. It hadn't been until her teen years that she'd begun to blossom, and by then she'd learned to value and depend on her personality rather than her looks.

Still, she knew others were moved by her appearance: the hormone-driven boys at school, the judges for homecoming queen in college and, later, men at work. And sometimes she couldn't help wondering where Aiden fell, if perhaps he'd chosen her because he'd seen her as a trophy wife.

The sound of a file drawer opening drew her out of her bleak thoughts. "What was I working on when I had my accident?"

"I'm not entirely sure."

"Didn't I talk to you about my work?"

Jill swallowed. "Well, yes, but not as much as you used to before the baby came along."

Aiden flicked through the files. He didn't seem happy with that answer. A muscle bunched along his jaw.

"Why don't you just look around? Maybe something will jar your memory. I'll just sit over here, out of the way." She pulled a novel out of her bag. "Take your time."

About two hours later Jill looked up from her book. Aiden had spent much of that time exploring: opening drawers, riffling their contents, lifting blinds and examining the view. He'd also paced to the hall and back several times, run his fingers over every touchable surface, and sniffed the air from every conceivable vantage point. Finally he'd settled in his leather chair with a stack of files. He was still reading.

"What *are* you doing?" Jill asked him.

He looked up. His hair was mussed, and his eyes looked tired. "Studying. If I can't remember what I did for a living, the least I can do is relearn it."

Her eyes widened. "You're studying your files?"

He gave a sheepish shrug. "Don't knock it. I think I could almost fake my way through."

"You're an intelligent man, Aiden," she said, although *intelligent* was an understatement, "but not even you can make up ten years' worth of experience by reading files."

He sighed, dragging his hand down his face. "I suppose you're right. Maybe we should go home. I'm not getting much accomplished here."

Jill slipped on her jacket and gathered up her purse. She was perplexed by her ambivalent reaction. She was disappointed for Aiden, of course. He was working so hard to get better. But she was also relieved.

She was walking behind him through the outer office when an absurd thought struck her. What if he remained this way forever? What if he never remembered anything about his work? The thought wasn't nearly as unpleasant as it should have been.

Aiden had just locked the door and they were turning to walk to the elevator, when his flow of movement came to an abrupt halt. He even stopped breathing. Jill shot him a look of alarm, wondering if he was in any physical pain.

"I remember you," he whispered. She noticed he was gazing over the mezzanine railing down on the pit. He laughed quite abruptly. "I remember."

Jill clutched her purse to her chest. Her heart pounded. Was this the moment the interlude ended? "What exactly do you remember?"

"Seeing you for the first time. I was standing on this very spot." He looked from the workstations below to her, his face flushing with animation. "You worked here!" he said, realizing it finally.

"Yes." She smiled.

His eyes glittered. "I was standing here talking with Joe Malone when I noticed you. I'd just returned from a trip to Japan, and while I was gone you'd been hired. You were on the phone, and you had your legs crossed and your skirt hiked up to heaven and—" he laughed again "—I felt like I'd been hit by an eighteen-wheeler."

"You what?"

"I was bowled over. Knocked out cold. Road kill on the highway of love."

Jill laughed. "You? Mr. Cool-calm-and-collected?"

"Absolutely."

He'd never told her that before. Her lips got quivery and twitchy with a giddy smile. She wiped her hand across her mouth and tried to think more sobering thoughts.

"Aiden, do you realize you just remembered Joe Malone?"

"Hmm. So I did." He tilted his head. He seemed interested for about three seconds before his attention returned to her. "I remember I used to come out here every chance I got just to watch you. You lit up the pit, Jill, you and your blond hair and long legs and short skirts."

Jill felt her neck warming. "You were checking out my legs all those times you were standing here?"

"Yes. And other assets."

Flattered in spite of herself, she leaned back, resting her elbows on the balustrade, and aimed a flirtatious grin at Aiden. "And here I was thinking you were watching me because I was new and you were checking on my work."

"Oh, I did that, too." Aiden stepped closer. "Mostly I couldn't believe that someone as gorgeous as you could also be so good. You were efficient and smart and naturally vivacious on the phone with customers."

"Now you tell me. The first time you called me into your office I thought you were going to fire me."

"And instead I offered you a promotion to be my assistant." He moved closer still, his left hand on the railing now so that she felt corralled. She didn't mind at all.

"Yes. It was outrageous. I went from entry-level sales to corporate assistant in three weeks. Everyone hated me." Jill met his eyes, feeling again the excitement of those early days of their relationship.

"What can I say?" Aiden smiled down at her lazily. "When I see something I want, I go after it."

"Yeah, well—" her voice shook under the influence of that smile "—I didn't know. According to the office grapevine, you weren't into serious involvements, and you never mixed dating and business."

"I wasn't, and didn't—until you."

His eyes locked on Jill's, and her heart soared and expanded. Suddenly she felt she was falling in love for the first time, all over again.

But even as she was basking in the heady feeling, she could see that Aiden's grasp on the past was slipping. He backed off slightly and scratched his forehead, frowning. "How did we make the transition from a work relationship to dating? I can't seem to recall."

"I worked as your assistant for a week. I went to my first board meeting with you and got to run the projector."

Aiden blinked. "My slides. The electronics factory in Tokyo."

"Yes." Jill swallowed, remembering that week as the toughest of her life. She'd fallen so head over heels for him she couldn't think straight.

She gazed at Aiden now and her traitorous heart turned over. Physically he was still the same overpoweringly handsome man and she was the same woman, drawn to him on a level that cut through reason and all common sense.

"And then what?" Aiden asked softly, his gaze moving over her face, caressing each feature, lingering on her mouth before returning to her eyes.

"Then one evening when we were working late, you—" she wet her parched lips "—kissed me."

"Just like that?" Aiden's voice was soft, and much too near. Heat began pulsing from her body in waves she was sure he could detect. Yet she was unable to draw away from him.

"Well, not out of the blue. I think we'd been thinking about it all week. At least I had." Jill was finding it hard to speak, hard to string her words together.

"It must've been quite a kiss—" his breath feathered over her cheek "—if we'd been building up to it for a week."

Jill shivered. Aiden wasn't even touching her, and she tingled all over. "It was just a kiss," she lied.

"Maybe if you refreshed my memory..." Aiden's left arm encircled her, exerting the slightest pressure to draw her closer.

"Aiden, your cast." She backed away.

"Is it hurting you?" He lifted his right arm to the side so that it wasn't touching her at all, anywhere.

"Yes. Um... No. I don't want to hurt *you.*"

"You're not." The corner of his mouth lifted in a heart-stopping smile. "You're not," he repeated in a whisper, bringing his arm down again, gently, behind her back. His other arm was already there, which meant, she realized fuzzily, she was in Aiden's arms. His free hand slid upward, under her hair, sending a cascade of delicious sensations shuddering through her.

He was dipping his head to kiss her when Jill finally found a thread of common sense. She turned to avoid his lips, and he nuzzled the sensitive area behind her ear instead. Her knees nearly buckled.

"Hmm," he murmured. "I really think it would do my memory a world of good if you'd kiss me, Jill."

"Boy, I've heard some lines..." she tried to quip. But her light remark did nothing to deter Aiden. He wound a hank of her long hair around his fingers and gently turned her head so that she had to face him. The next moment his mouth had covered hers.

If Jill began the kiss with resistance, only seconds elapsed before that changed. Aiden's lips were too warm and far too pleasurable. Before she realized it, something ignited within her, and she was kissing him back, urgently, with the hunger of someone too long denied.

They shouldn't be doing this, she told herself. They were caught in a time warp, frozen at a moment when their love was new and exciting and unspoiled. For all she knew, Aiden's memory might come crashing back in its entirety tomorrow, and with it would come the aloof, career-driven man who'd killed that love.

Jill was embarrassed to realize it was Aiden who broke from the kiss first. "Ah, yes. Now it's coming back," he murmured, his eyes gleaming, attractive creases fanning from their outer corners. "We kissed and I told you I wanted to start seeing you outside the office. Our first date was dinner at an Italian restaurant. Boston's north end. Right?"

"Yes." Pushing against his chest, Jill put a few inches between them. "I spilled my wine."

"And I reminded you it was good luck. Was I right? Did it turn out to be good luck? I can't seem to remember." The gleam in his eyes turned roguish. "I probably need more reminding."

"Oh, Aiden," she chided, but even she knew it was a lost cause. He was charming and disarming, and she'd been charmed and disarmed.

He kissed her again, longer, more intimately than the

first time, and Jill didn't even try to resist. She let herself be swept away.

"Yes, I remember," he said a bit raggedly when he eventually lifted his head. "It was definitely good luck. Two weeks later I asked you to marry me, and you said yes."

Against her better judgment, memories of their whirlwind courtship flooded her, sweeping her back. He'd sent her flowers every day and hired a limo to drive her to and from work so she wouldn't have to take the train. One weekend he even chartered a private plane and flew them to Maine, to a quiet, romantic inn on the coast.

But do you know him, Jill?

"Aiden, did you love me?" she asked unexpectedly, surprising even herself.

Aiden's face dropped. "What sort of question is that?"

She stepped away from him. "It's just...I've sometimes wondered."

"All the time we were dating, I never told you I loved you?"

She was relieved he'd interpreted her question as referring to the beginning of their relationship only.

"You did. Of course you did," she assured him, staring at his shirt collar rather than meeting his eyes.

"But?" he prodded.

"But not often and never in...passion. You were such a careful person. Private, quiet, always in control. I was never sure you meant it."

Aiden turned, propping his elbow on the balustrade, his chin in his hand.

He slanted a glance her way. "Careful, huh?"

She nodded. "There was a part of you that you always kept off-limits, even to me."

"Jill, men are notoriously bad at expressing feelings."

"I know," she agreed. "I know." But her voice betrayed her lingering reservations.

"Tell me." He turned to her. There was an openness, an accessibility, in his eyes she'd only seen in her dreams.

"I always felt your reticence went beyond what was normal for men. It was a deliberate guardedness, as if you were purposely hiding from me. You gave with your body, but I never felt I really knew who you were, how you felt deep down."

What she didn't tell him was, she'd felt that way throughout their marriage. Something vital had always seemed missing. Trust, she supposed. He'd never trusted her enough to let her into his innermost feelings.

"Why are you telling me this now?"

"I'm not sure. I sense you're approachable tonight."

"And you'll get an honest answer?"

"Yes. Strange, isn't it?"

"Very." His brow tightened.

They stood for a long while, staring at the industrial-grade gray carpeting, lost in thought. Eventually Jill asked, "How well do you remember that time in our lives?"

He rubbed his hand over his forehead. "It seems pretty clear. I'm not sure, though."

"Do you remember how precisely you pictured your future?"

He kept rubbing his brow as if trying to coax out the elusive memories. "I can't seem to recall. Sorry."

"You had it all planned out. The kind of house you wanted to live in, the sort of entertaining we'd do, how often we'd travel, and where. Everything. And it was on a timetable. By the age of thirty-five you expected to be...well, never mind." Let him remember that on his own.

"My point is, I've sometimes thought I was on your

timetable, too. It was the right time for you to marry, and so you looked around and there I was. A year earlier you wouldn't have noticed me."

Aiden gazed at her, suppressing a grin. "Oh, I doubt that very much, Jill."

"Are you sure? You once told me you'd begun to feel odd at parties where all the other executives were married. It also occurred to me that being settled and appearing stable could be important to your career."

Aiden brushed back a lock of her hair and tucked it behind her ear. The way his eyes gleamed, she sensed he wasn't taking this too seriously anymore. "Go on. Don't stop now."

"I also know you checked out my background. My looks had already passed muster evidently, but you needed to see what the rest of me was like."

"Seems I liked what I found." His eyes swept downward, heating her in places she didn't want to be warmed.

"What was not to like?" she said sardonically. "I went to private schools, came from a solid, upper-middle-class family—church-goers, all. My father was a conservative with his own small business and membership in an exclusive country club. My brother was an Eagle Scout, and my mother volunteered and entertained." Jill slumped, dejected. "I was perfect."

After a while, Aiden said, "Are you finished?"

A long sigh. "Yes."

"Good. First of all, I'm not sure if I had a timetable, Jill. I might have. I seem to be that kind of guy. But I am sure I didn't put you on it in any calculated way. You completely bowled me over. I told you that."

Jill peeked at him through peevishly lowered lashes. "Really?"

"Really. I was so taken with you I needed a compass just to find the water cooler."

A smile began to tug at her mouth.

"Second, your background didn't 'pass muster'," he mocked.

Jill swiveled toward him, offended. "Why not?"

"I really didn't want to get involved with someone who wasn't from the area."

Her heart beat noticeably faster. "Do you remember where I was from?"

"Sure. A suburb of Cincinnati. You came to Boston to attend college—like I did. When I met you, you were living with a roommate in a basement apartment in Cambridge, doing the eager-career-girl thing. But you'd come from a great family, and I was afraid you'd get to missing them someday and decide to go back home."

"You were afraid I'd leave you because I missed my family?"

"Yes. Especially your parents. Mildred. Charles." Aiden paused and blew out a long sigh. "They were a hard act to follow."

He touched his hand to her cheek, stroking it with his thumb. "Maybe I was too careful, Jill. Maybe I was methodical and had certain expectations. But aside from all that, I also loved you. That's why I married you." He looked straight into her eyes, right into her soul. "Don't ever doubt that I loved you," he said emphatically.

From down the mezzanine, the elevator hummed. The doors glided open, and the security guard stepped out. "Oh. I was just coming to see if you were still here," he said when he spotted Jill and Aiden.

They stepped apart.

"Will you be staying much later? I go off shift now, and I just..."

Aiden fit his arm around Jill's waist. "No. We're heading out." He smiled faintly. "I've done enough...catching up for one night."

* * *

That night Jill flopped into bed, exhausted in body but mentally wired. When the time had come for Aiden to turn in, he'd mentioned he could probably manage the stairs and start sleeping in their room again. She'd convinced him to continue using the guest room, but she didn't know how much longer she could put him off.

But that was only part of the concerns keeping Jill awake. Aiden's recollections also bothered her. He'd told her he'd felt as if he'd been hit by a truck when he'd first laid eyes on her. Bowled over. And he'd asserted that, without a doubt, he'd loved her.

Why hadn't he told her those wonderful things then, when they were happening? Why had he kept his feelings locked so tight?

As the numerals on the bedside digital clock progressed into the wee hours, an odd thought struck her. All these years she'd doubted Aiden's love, and yet, not only had it existed, it had been intense. He'd just kept it hidden. Was it possible that he'd hidden other emotions from her, as well? Love for their daughter, for instance? Could it have been there all along?

Jill stared into the darkness over her bed, plagued by another mystery. Why was he free to let that love flow now? Why was he able to express his feelings? In wiping out his episodic memory, had the plane accident wiped out something that kept his guardedness in place?

Her head ached. She was thinking too much. Dr. Grogan had probably gotten it right when he'd said being free of job responsibilities was the thing making Aiden more relaxed and open. She shouldn't read anything more into it.

Punching up the pillow, Jill turned on her side and tried to clear her mind. But then she remembered the kisses she and Aiden had shared tonight. Her body remembered, too, stirring and warming with a mind all its own.

She should've prevented those kisses. Now what was she going to do? What can of peas had she opened?

She should've and *could've* prevented those kisses, but strangely she hadn't. The truth of the matter was, she'd enjoyed being in Aiden's arms again, she liked how he was acting, and she loved living the pretense that they were happily married.

A thought she'd had earlier sneaked into her mind. What if Aiden's memory never returned? What if he stayed just as he was now forever, frozen in his obliviously romantic time warp? It was a possibility, wasn't it? She was sure she'd read of amnesia patients lingering, uncured, for years.

On that thought, Jill closed her eyes and smiled. A few minutes later she was sound asleep.

CHAPTER SIX

AS SOON as Jill looked into Aiden's study the next morning, she knew something had happened overnight. She'd gone to sleep on a dream of Aiden remaining in his obliviousness forever, but watching him now, she knew it was a dream that wasn't meant to be.

His computer was running. So was the modem and the laser printer. Papers lay sprawled on his desk. And in the midst of it all stood Aiden, so engrossed he hadn't even taken the time to dress or shave.

Seeing her father, Maddy began to squirm in Jill's arms and ask to be put down. *Down* was her latest new word.

Aiden looked away from the computer screen and broke into a smile. "Hey, how's my girl? Come here, sweetheart."

Jill set Maddy on her feet, and she toddled into the study, a room that had hitherto been off-limits. Her steps were still unsteady, her balance precarious, and before she got even halfway to Aiden, she gave up on walking for the more familiar and secure mode of travel—crawling.

Aiden crouched and, using his left arm, scooped her up. "Good morning, Madison Kay," he said, giving her three noisy kisses on the cheek.

Jill stood in the doorway, watching them, her throat tightening and her eyes growing hot, a condition that seemed to be turning chronic of late. Aiden looked at her over their daughter's soft blond curls, his eyes warm and magnetic and saying good morning in a more intimate way.

"What's happened?" she asked meaningfully, leaning against the door frame and folding her arms.

"It was the strangest thing," Aiden said on a chuckle. He sat in his leather chair, settling Maddy on his lap. "I opened my eyes this morning, and there it was. The files and reports I couldn't make heads or tails of at my office last night? I knew exactly what they were about." Maddy patted his unshaven chin. He kissed her hand.

"That's great." Jill meant to be happy for him—and she was—but she also felt robbed. It wasn't a pleasant sensation. She stared at the computer screen, resenting it. But, of course, it wasn't the computer's fault. Time was restoring Aiden's memory; time, destroying the fantasy she'd come to love.

She thought about the intimacy she and Aiden had shared the night before, and knew for certain she should've prevented it, if not for Aiden's sake, then for her own. She was going to be hurt when this was over. Unfortunately the damage had already been done. But that didn't mean it had to get worse. With self-control and determination she could guarantee it didn't.

"That was just the beginning." Aiden swiveled and rocked the chair for his daughter's entertainment. "I was lying there, thinking about one particular file, and suddenly I realized I remembered other things about work. Lots of other things." He shook his head, amazed. "It was as if a door had opened while I was asleep."

"Just like that." Jill tried to be amazed, too, but she couldn't help thinking the whole idea was a bit scary. Instead of seeing it as doors opening, she saw chunks of memory coming back like bombs, exploding when least expected.

"Yep. Just like that. So you see, going to the office really did help."

Aiden pulled a handkerchief out of his robe pocket and wiped the baby's chin.

"I think she's teething again," Jill said to explain Maddy's drooling.

"Do we have any paregoric in the house?"

Paregoric? Where had he picked *that* up? Jill should've been used to these disjointed moments by now, but she wasn't. They still made her look at Aiden as if he'd dropped in from another planet.

"Uh...no. The pediatrician recommended another product. I'll rub some on her gums later."

Jill pushed away from the door frame and stepped into the room. "So, what are you doing now?" she asked, glowering at the humming printer.

"One of the things I awoke remembering was that this computer's connected to the system at work. I've just been retrieving some reports, leaving messages for people and instructions for my secretary—that sort of thing."

Jill went to the window that looked out on the tennis court. "You remember people at work, too?"

"Yes. It's a complete package, that portion of my memory that's returned. My job, the work I was doing, the people around me."

Maddy slid off Aiden's lap and tugged at the bottom drawer of his desk. She probably thought she could explore these drawers the way she did the drawers and cupboards in the kitchen.

"Oh, honey, don't do that," Jill said, hurrying forward.

"It's okay." Aiden waved Jill off. Surprisingly, he helped Maddy open the drawer. Instead of important papers or valuable office supplies, Jill saw it was filled with unbreakable odds and ends: a tennis ball, a trio of stacking cups, a pack of playing cards, spoons, and lots of other items she couldn't yet make out.

She was still trying to adjust to her surprise, when the other emotions struck, emotions she wished she weren't experiencing—tenderness toward Aiden and an excruciating melancholy for a situation that wouldn't last. For if he remembered work, his myopic dedication to it would soon follow, and how long after that before he locked out his family, from this room and from his life?

"I suppose you'll be wanting to go into the office soon," Jill said, already feeling the emptiness of the house without him. She waited, teeth clenched, for him to say yes, he was ready now.

"Hell, no!" Aiden reached out, caught her wrist and pulled her toward him. Jill was so surprised by his answer, her legs gave out and she fell rather gracelessly into his lap.

"I have some free time coming to me," he said. "I'm going to enjoy it with my family, every last minute, and maybe then some."

She braced herself against the back of the chair to protect his broken arm. Or maybe it was herself she was trying to protect. Dressed only in his robe, Aiden was far too accessible.

With one hand lightly resting at her waist, he traced her jawline with the other. "What do you think of the idea of stealing away somewhere for a while?"

Her eyes snapped wide open. "Who? When?"

She must've looked totally flummoxed because Aiden chuckled. "You, me, the baby. In a couple of days, right after I see Grogan."

"Where do you want to go?"

Aiden shrugged casually. "I found some vacation brochures for Cape Cod in a file marked 'Travel'. Seems we've been there, but I'm afraid I don't remember. Do you think that would be a good place to go?"

"Yes!" Jill replied with enthusiasm. "There won't be any summer tourists there yet. We'll have the beach all to ourselves."

"Great. I'll make reservations today." Aiden slid his

fingers into her hair and drew her closer. "Have I told you lately how beautiful you look in the morning?" He didn't give her a chance to answer.

His lips touched hers, brushing them, warming them with such a light touch, yet she felt reverberations throughout her body. In her tightening breasts, the pit of her stomach, her weakening thighs. Before she'd even thought about it, she'd leaned into him, seeking more. His arms tightened around her as he angled his mouth and took her more possessively.

She utterly melted. Her hands moved to his shoulders, her fingers pressing into hard muscle as desire spiraled within her. Against his chest her heart thudded with hard, quickened strokes.

The volatility of her response to Aiden had the opposite effect of startling her to her senses. Where was that willpower she'd been so certain she had? How had she let this happen again? Exerting a great deal of self-discipline, Jill pushed away and, laboring for breath, asked, "What would you like for breakfast?"

Aiden grinned, his twinkling eyes answering, *You.*

She half groaned, half chuckled, fighting off her chagrin. "I can't believe I said that." She levered herself off his lap.

He held on to her hand and gave it a gentle tug. "What's your hurry?"

Jill cast their daughter a glance. "Maddy..."

"Is fine."

And she was. She was engrossed in emptying the desk drawer that Aiden had purposely filled for her. Jill searched for a different excuse, but Aiden didn't give her time to find one.

"Jill, what's going on?"

She turned. He was studying her with narrowed, penetrating eyes. Her stomach clenched. "What do you mean?"

"Why the distance between us, the reluctance on your part to be intimate? You didn't want me upstairs last night and now you can't wait to leave me to make breakfast. It can't still be because of Maddy's birthday." He attempted a smile. "Even you couldn't hold a grudge that long."

Heat washed through Jill, deepening her chagrin. She hadn't expected him to pick up on her attitude so soon. And even when he had, she didn't expect him to confront her so openly.

"Is it the memory-loss thing again?" He seemed hurt and more than concerned. "Do you feel uneasy because I still don't remember you beyond our earliest days together?"

She felt torn up. Guilt and anxiety told her she ought to educate him to the facts of the matter, that he wasn't really a man who'd choose to stay home with his family when he could go to work instead. Nor were they in the habit of starting their day in his study, cuddling and kissing. They were, in fact, on the verge of divorce. That was what she ought to tell him.

"What is it, Jill?" Aiden probed. "Are you unhappy with me? Is something wrong with our marriage?"

Tell him, her conscience urged. *He isn't going to thank you for procrastinating when his memory comes back.*

But her courage failed her. Or maybe it was simply selfishness that took over. She was enjoying the fantasy too much. Maybe tomorrow...

Leaning forward, she placed a kiss on the corner of his mouth. "No, Aiden. Nothing's wrong with our marriage."

He sighed in relief, believing her, and for a moment she knew how it felt to be a Judas.

People at ABX began responding to Aiden's communications by 9:05. By 10:15 he hadn't even shaved yet. Getting off the phone from his sixth call, Aiden stepped out of his study and let out a yowl Jill heard even upstairs with the vacuum cleaner running.

"What did I start?" He walked up the stairs, climbed over the safety gate at the top and, entering their bedroom, turned off the vacuum. "Where's the baby's backpack, Jill?"

"Right where I left it when I came in from her walk yesterday. The front closet. Why?"

"Come on. We're getting out of here."

They started their walk at the pond, where they threw stale bread to the ducks who inhabited the reeds along the shoreline. Jill was glad to get out of the house. Here in the open, there was little risk of intimacy between her and Aiden.

After a short stroll along the pond, they took to the woods. The air was cool, only in the middle fifties, and the sky above the barely budded trees was overcast. But they were dressed warmly, and the woods held too many treasures for them to even think of turning back: wild hollies, pussy willows, mosses and lichens growing on old stone walls.

Maddy rode along in the backpack, contented throughout. Jill sometimes thought her daughter could spend the entire day that way, provided the back she was riding on didn't give out.

Jill's one worry was that trekking over uneven ground would do fresh damage to Aiden's newly healed ankle. But he assured her that the pair of old hiking boots he was wearing supported him like armor.

"Are you sure Maddy's not becoming too heavy for you?" Jill asked, stepping along a winding path she'd often walked before, sometimes alone, sometimes with her friend Eric, but never with Aiden. She wanted nothing to detract from his first visit to her woods. "I can take over if you're getting tired."

"Jill, she barely weighs twenty-five pounds. She's fine. I'm fine. Stop hovering."

"Sorry."

He angled a grin her way. "Don't be. I love it."

He tried to hold her gaze, but she looked away, determined to deny the hum of awareness buzzing between them.

"So, continue," she reminded him. He'd been relaying to her other memories he'd awakened with that morning. Memories involving her. He wasn't sure if they were right or he'd just dreamed them up, and claimed he needed her verification.

"I seem to recall you had an unusual college record. You started out majoring in business then switched over and got your degree in something totally different." He shot her a questioning glance.

"Right. Art appreciation. I wasn't cut out for business."

"Why'd you start with it, then? Your father's influence?"

"Uh-uh. My mother's."

"Mildred's?" Aiden almost choked. "Are we talking about the same woman whose aim in life is to win the intergalactic award for domestic perfection?"

"The same." Jill smiled. In spite of herself, she was enjoying Aiden's interest in her. She felt...courted. "My mother said it was the best way to find a husband. Business classes would be filled with eligible young men."

Aiden threw back his head and laughed. Jill loved the deep, rich sound.

"I have to ask, with a degree in art appreciation, how did you end up at ABX?"

Jill lifted aside a low tree branch. "I was unemployed.

The rent was due. I saw an ad in *The Globe* for ABX. I applied and was hired on the strength of my two years as a business major. It was that simple."

Aiden walked along easily, his scuffed boots kicking up dry winter leaves. "Fate, then."

"Fate?"

"That brought us together."

Jill chewed on a bemused smile. Aiden, speaking of fate. Would he ever stop surprising her?

"It's ironic that my meeting you came about indirectly because of my mother's advice. Finding a husband was the last thing on my mind when I applied for a job at ABX."

"You were good at it, Jill. If you'd stayed..."

"That's another irony. I thought I wanted to be a career girl. It's so...expected these days. As it turns out, I'm a throwback to another generation. I love being a housewife and mother."

"And I, for one, am glad." Aiden slipped his hand under the collar of her jacket and drew her closer. Somehow the move seemed as intimate as a kiss.

"Are you sure? You don't think I've become frumpy and unexciting?" She was amazed by how easily she was sharing her doubts, doubts that had plagued her privately for so long.

"Oh, yeah." Aiden rolled his eyes. "I think you're a dog."

Jill didn't want to feel anything, but his compliment sent a thrill zinging through her. Still smiling, she said, "I once saw a T-shirt with the slogan, 'Mirror, mirror, on the wall. I'm my mother, after all'."

Aiden laughed, attractive lines etching his face.

"Being your mother isn't such a bad thing. Mildred's okay."

"I got the feeling you didn't like her, the few times you met her."

"She just scared me. So did your father, for that matter. And the house you grew up in. Everything about them was so perfect."

Jill stopped walking. "Why did that scare you?"

Aiden lifted one broad shoulder. "I felt like a fraud. My own background was so different."

As they resumed walking, Jill realized her pulse rate had picked up. She wasn't sure if she was excited over the fact that Aiden was confiding in her, or over the possibility he'd remembered more of his past, details he'd never shared with her before.

"Aiden, while you were in the hospital, you remembered that you'd come to Boston to attend college. You even remembered the guys you roomed with and some of your classes."

"Yes."

"Do you remember *why* you chose Boston? Where you came from? Your family?"

They walked several yards, Aiden's brow furrowed deeply. Finally he shook his head, looking discouraged.

"Never mind," she said softly.

They paused to examine what appeared to be a fox hole, then continued walking, relaxing again into the peace of a simple stroll in the woods. Occasionally, however, Jill noticed him looking up at the trees, tilting his head, as if they were whispering to him.

Abruptly he came to a stop. "I have a sense of growing up in the Pacific northwest."

Jill tensed. He looked at her and she nodded that he was right. "Is it the trees?"

"Yeah. There were so many. A forest." He rubbed his hand across his eyes. "That's where my mother lives."

Jill's heart ached. "I'm sorry, Aiden. Your mother died several years ago, well before we met." She hated giving him the news, but better now than have him build up expectations.

"Are you sure?"

"Yes. You told me so yourself." She touched his cheek, which she thought unusually pale. "Do you remember our wedding?"

"Uh-huh."

"Was she there?"

He swallowed, then shook his head.

They resumed walking, the heavy silence disturbed only by the crunch of twigs and leaves underfoot.

"My father's gone, too," Aiden said unexpectedly.

"That's right. He wasn't at our wedding, either."

"No, I remember...from before."

Jill's gaze shot to him. "From before?"

"Yeah. I lived with him in San Francisco. He clerked in a hardware store there. Probably where I got my business sense."

Jill already knew he'd lived with his father after the divorce, but he'd never told her any of the particulars.

"Had your mother already passed away?" she asked experimentally.

Aiden's expression became painfully inward-looking. "I don't see her there, San Francisco. I think they...they were divorced. I can't see that far back, though—you know, to them separating. I don't think I like looking back."

Jill understood. "Can you see the house you and your father lived in?"

"It wasn't a house. It was an apartment. Up some stairs. Yes, I remember now." He nodded and smiled, and Jill breathed a little easier.

Stepping over a log, she asked, "What was he like, your father?"

Aiden opened his mouth, paused, then snapped it shut again. "I honestly don't know. He and I didn't talk a whole helluva lot. When he came in from the store, he washed up and ate, then sat in front of the TV until it was time for bed. His name was John."

Lulled by the walking and talking, Maddy had laid her head against her father's shoulder. Jill smiled, watching the pink pompon on her knit hat bobbing with each stride Aiden took. God, she hoped this child grew up remembering more than just her father's name.

Returning her attention to Aiden, she asked, "While your father did his thing, what kept you occupied?"

"Oh..." Aiden squinted up at the trees. "I played a lot of basketball. There was a playground just up the street."

"Sounds nice."

He breathed out a scornful laugh. "It was, once you let the drug dealers know you weren't interested." The flow and tone of his words had taken on an assurance that indicated he was seeing that part of his life with increasing clarity.

"But then my father died, my first year of high school, and I had to go live with my uncle."

"Your uncle?" Jill's head swiveled. She'd never heard anything about an uncle.

"Yeah. Benny. My father's younger brother. He lived in San Francisco, too, though we weren't really all that close."

Jill surmised Aiden's mother had died by then, since he hadn't gone back to live with her. "Sounds like you weren't crazy about living with your uncle."

"I wasn't. Benny had five kids already and barely enough income to keep food on *their* plates."

"I hope he didn't make you feel unwanted, Aiden. Good Lord, you were what—fourteen? And your father just recently gone."

Aiden's mouth took a wry twist. "Finesse wasn't exactly Benny's strong suit. Nor his wife's. They were rough-cut people, soured on life. Impatient. Spoke at a decibel level that could've shattered concrete, and most of what they said was, 'Get out of my way, kid,' not just to me, their own children, as well."

"Oh, Aiden." Jill's heart ached for him.

Aiden only shrugged. "I survived. Spent lots of time away from the house, walking the streets, sitting in the library." His usually well-modulated voice had taken on a hollow flatness that spoke volumes about the loneliness of that time in his life.

"Couldn't you have lived with someone else?"

"There was no one else, and I sure as hell didn't want to be placed in a foster home. I already felt I had no control over my life, what with my parents' divorce and my being moved around and then my father dying."

"And leaving you in the care of an uncle who didn't love or want you."

Aiden nodded, agreeing. "I didn't need a social service agency jumping into the act and running my life, too. And at least Benny was family."

They'd already begun to head back. Jill could see a speck of clearing through the trees in the distance.

"I stayed with Benny three years. By then I had a job and could afford to move out. I lived in a rooming house my last year of high school." Inadvertently he grimaced, and Jill could only imagine what that rooming house had been like.

"And then you came east to college, and the rest, as they say, is history." Lips pressed tight, Jill shook her head.

"It really wasn't so bad. Lots of people've had it worse—though I vowed if I ever got away, I'd never go back. Not to that city. Not to that poverty. Not to that loneliness."

To herself Jill added, *and never again to being at the mercy of others.* That was probably the underlying reason he'd gone into management. Why he was so driven to be top dog, as well. He needed to feel in control of the circumstances of his life. And little wonder, considering his background.

The only mystery to her was how far Aiden had come from where he'd been.

"You know," she said, smiling sympathetically, "my parents wouldn't have driven you off if you'd told them your background. Just the opposite. I think it would've impressed them. It's a testament to your ambition and intelligence."

"Well, let's just say I wasn't going to take any chances."

"Does anyone at ABX know?"

"No. Nobody needs to know. This is who I am now."

Jill sighed incredulously, thinking it had taken her three years but she finally knew her husband.

They left the woods, coming out one house up from theirs. Throughout their walk the air had been thickening with moisture. Now it was condensing into mist.

"Looks like we're in for some rain," Jill remarked.

"I think you're right." But instead of looking up at the sky, Aiden gave the woods a backward glance, as if they were still whispering to him.

By the time they reached the house, their clothing was damp and their bodies chilled. Jill took off Maddy's jacket and hat, then bundled her in an extra-warm sweater.

"Look how rosy her cheeks are," she commented on a chuckle.

"Mmm. We have ourselves one healthy kid there," he said proudly.

Jill noticed he was struggling to take off his boots. "Here, let me help." She'd had to help him into the boots, too. Lacing ties was one job that was still beyond him. So was getting the backpack on and off.

She knelt in front of him and loosened the thick, damp laces of his right boot and tugged it off his foot. Then she repeated the process with his other boot, taking it off more gently. Propping that foot on her thigh, she lightly massaged his ankle. It seemed to have swelled again. Under her hands his wool-socked foot was heavy and large. A man's foot. She suddenly had the urge to press her cheek to it.

Softly she asked, "How's your ankle feeling?"

He didn't answer. Curious, she glanced up and realized he was watching her, his ankle probably the last thing on his mind. She tried to look away but couldn't. He held her mesmerized, drawing her into him with the intensity of his longing. The space between them began to throb with messages of heat and need.

Aiden's mouth lifted fractionally and his eyes crinkled, acknowledging the spell they'd woven, and breaking it, all at the same time. Releasing a held breath, Jill got off her knees, took a thick sweatshirt off the peg by the door and slipped it on.

"Are you cold?" he asked. "I'll lay a fire."

"We can turn up the heat just as easily."

Aiden's lips twitched. "We can do that too, later. Right now I think I'll just build a fire."

Trying to ignore his innuendo, she said, "Great. I'll put on some soup."

They ate their lunch—steaming bowls of barley soup with crusty French bread and herb-seasoned butter—by the fireplace in the family room. Afterward, Jill took Maddy up to her room and settled her in for a nap.

Returning to the family room, she found Aiden setting up the chess board on the pine coffee table on which they'd feasted. Something soft was playing on the stereo.

"Can I challenge you to a game?" he asked.

"If you want to lose your shirt."

He responded with a raised eyebrow and a hint of a smile.

"Don't say it," she warned, heading off another double entendre.

Laughing, he patted the floor beside him.

They played their game to the peaceful sounds of the hissing fire and the quiet music—and Maddy's restful breathing through the monitor. Outside, the mist thickened. Inside, shadows deepened. They didn't talk much. They didn't have to. They were in perfect accord.

Jill looked up from the game board. Firelight flickered over Aiden's face, dark here, light there, enhancing features that were already perfect. Although he still needed a shave and his hair was standing in swirls, she'd never seen him looking more handsome, or more relaxed. She wondered if the walk through the woods had done it, or the talk.

A pleasurable warmth slid through her as she pictured him again, speaking about his past, confiding in her, finally letting her in. She still didn't like his obsessive drive on the job, but at least now she understood it, and anything was tolerable when it was understood.

"Your move," he reminded her gently.

"Oh." She glided her rook forward, taking one of his bishops. He huddled over the board, his thumb stroking his bottom lip and rasping softly on his beard.

As pleased as she was by today's disclosures, she couldn't help but feel downhearted, too. Another segment of his memory had returned. Now he'd filled in most of the blanks from late childhood onward: living with his father, the years with his uncle, college, going to work at ABX, meeting her and getting married. Some areas were still quite sketchy, but at least the general framework was there. Only his earliest and very latest years were completely missing, but Jill knew it would only be a matter of time. And when that final bomb went off, when he remembered their marriage and the fact it was over, this charade of peace and happiness would be over, as well.

Aiden moved a pawn and looked up, catching her watching him. She was ashamed to realize there were tears in her eyes. "Jill?" He moved to her side of the table and slid his arm across her shoulders. "Hey. What's the matter?"

Her bottom lip quivered and a tear she tried to forestall rolled down her cheek. Suddenly she burst into a sobbing laugh. "This is a beautiful afternoon, isn't it?"

He looked at her as if she'd gone 'round the bend.

She laughed again, and another tear slid down the side of her nose. "It's the sort of afternoon that makes a person realize how precious every minute of life is."

The lines of Aiden's face softened, and he pulled her against him. "You're crazier than I am."

Her vision blurred and swam. No, she wasn't crazy. She just realized they were living on borrowed time. "Oh, Aiden," she wept, curling her arms around him. She held him so tight she trembled.

"What is it, sweetheart?"

I love you. Oh, how I love you! she thought. But the sentiment never made it past her lips. "Nothing," she whispered, easing her death grip. "I'm just acting foolish."

Aiden put enough space between them to look into her eyes. His own were cold sober. "How about we act foolish together, hmm?" With that he lowered his head and kissed her.

It was a kiss that began in tenderness but quickly turned hot and strong. Jill sank against him, powerless to fight the attraction between them any longer. He was her husband, the only man she'd ever given herself to, the only man she'd ever wanted. And right now she wanted him more than anything.

With one foot, Aiden shoved the coffee table, making room for them on the rug in front of the fire. Then, still kissing her, he tipped her onto her back.

"Oh, Jill. I've wanted to be with you like this all week," he rasped, his lips hovering just a breath above hers. "It's been such torment."

She lifted her head just enough to brush her lips across his. "Then don't waste another minute. Love me, Aiden. Love me."

His mouth came down on hers with a covetousness that took her breath away. She dug her fingers into his hair, deepening the kiss, and moaned as his exploration grew bolder. Already her body felt molten with need.

He moved his hand along her ribs in a caressing up-and-down motion, coming closer each time to her breast. When his hand finally moved over her, kneading each soft mound, she whimpered. He slid his hand under her sweater and deftly undid the front clasp of her bra. His touch to her skin shot a bolt of fire right to her center.

Through the mounting passion fogging her brain, Jill realized that Aiden was resting on the elbow of his broken arm, and that it was probably getting tired, if not downright painful. "Lie back," she whispered. "Let me do the work."

Watching her with smoky, half-closed eyes, Aiden rolled onto his back and positioned his cast-clad arm over his head—a man in surrender. The darkening sky outside had intensified the coziness of the fire inside, its light wrapping them in a cocoon of intimate warmth.

Bracing herself over him, Jill showered his face with small, loving kisses. His lips parted, but she deliberately avoided them. Instead, she followed the line of his jaw to the strong length of his neck. His skin was fever-hot and his pulse was beating hard. His musky fragrance dizzied her. When she moved her attention to his ear, he shivered.

Jill could stay away from his mouth no longer. Lifting herself over him, she captured it fully, reveling in the response she felt in his tightening body.

His hand combed through her hair. Hers undid the top button of his shirt. His tightened in her hair. Hers undid two more buttons. And then...

The phone rang.

Jill broke the seal of their kiss and groaned, falling to her side. Aiden laughed.

"Let the answering machine take it," he said, reaching for her again.

"Mmm," she agreed, resuming their kiss.

But when the caller began to leave his message, they broke apart again. It was someone from ABX.

"Maybe you'd better answer that." Jill sat up. "It might be important."

Groaning, Aiden sat up, too. "I suppose you're right." He started to get up, but then changed his mind. The next moment, Jill was being kissed so lushly she lost all track of time or place or telephones. Finally, looking at her with desire-heavy eyes and a grin that curled her toes, he said, "Hold that thought." Then he answered the call.

Jill held the thought, but with one thing leading to another, she and Aiden never did return to the rug or their kisses. The fire died out and Maddy woke up and then it was time for dinner.

But neither of them forgot. For the rest of the day, every time they passed each other, every time they looked across a room, they promised. Tonight they'd be together.

There was no way Jill could put Aiden off any longer. First of all, she couldn't have, even if she'd wanted to. She hadn't a shred of resistance against the man. But second, she didn't want to.

For all she knew, this might be the last time she got

to hold him close, the last chance to know the heady fulfillment that came with loving him. She wasn't going to throw that chance away.

And who knew? Maybe this lovemaking would change things between them. Maybe, after Aiden was well again, they'd go for marriage counseling and rethink their decision to separate. Anything was possible. Right?

With dinner dishes done, Jill took Maddy upstairs for her bath, leaving Aiden in the garage tinkering with the engine in her car.

Maddy was splashing about in the warm, soapy water when the phone rang yet one more time. "Good grief," Jill complained, reaching for the phone on the bathroom wall.

"Hi, Jill?"

She sank to her knees beside the tub again. "Hi, Eric. Yes, I remembered. I'm supposed to be watching Brady tomorrow afternoon."

"Great, but that's not why I'm calling."

"Oh?" Jill filled a cup with water and poured it over her delighted daughter's tummy. "What's up?"

"Are you busy?"

"Sort of. I'm giving Maddy a bath."

"I won't be long, then. I just wanted you to know I got in touch with the lawyer who represented my ex in our divorce. You know, the man-eater I told you about."

"Yes."

"And she said she'd be happy to represent you."

Jill blinked, trying to get her mental focus back. After the day she'd spent with Aiden, the idea of separation and lawyers seemed light-years away. "I...um..."

"She's really good, Jill. Believe me, I know from bitter experience. She'll protect your interests well. And Maddy's."

"I haven't given it much thought since Aiden's accident."

"I understand. But you did ask me to call her. Remember?"

Now she did. Vaguely.

"She said you should give her office a ring as soon as possible. Got a pen handy?"

Jill suddenly felt rushed and confused.

"Oh, wait." She opened the top drawer of the vanity. The closest thing she found to a pen was an eyeliner pencil. "Go ahead." Eric read her the phone number and she jotted it on the corner of a tissue box, even though she strongly suspected she wasn't going to make the call.

Maddy had gotten to her feet and was walking in the tub.

"Sit down, honey," Jill said, afraid of her slipping. "Sit," she said more firmly. "Eric, I really have to go."

"Okay. Sorry for calling at such a bad time."

She was in the middle of saying, "Talk to you later," when she heard a strange click. She frowned, puzzled, because Eric was still on the line and just saying goodbye himself. *Then* he hung up.

She stared at the humming receiver, her heart pounding ever harder, her head so light she felt faint. *Oh, no!* she cried silently. *No!*

CHAPTER SEVEN

MAYBE she'd only imagined the click, Jill thought as she tiptoed down the stairs after tucking Maddy into her crib for the night. Or, if she had heard a click, maybe it was just static on the telephone line. Sure, that could be it. There was no logical reason for her to be jumping to the conclusion that it had been Aiden hanging up an extension.

But when Jill stepped into the kitchen and saw him waiting for her, she knew the click was neither static nor her imagination. It was, quite simply, her worst fear come true.

Aiden was sitting at the table in the breakfast nook, his shoulders uncharacteristically bowed. The lights were low, but she could still discern the pallor of his skin and the pain in his eyes.

Jill went to the sink and washed out Maddy's bottle. She could feel him following her with his eyes, following with his confusion and pain. She wished she were dead.

After putting away the bottle, she wiped down the counter, buying time. But, short of faking an appendicitis attack, she saw no way out of the confrontation.

She switched off the light over the sink, telling herself it wasn't going to be as bad as she thought; she and Aiden had come too far. Yet, when she crossed the kitchen, her legs were quivering.

"Okay, let's talk about it. You obviously overheard my conversation with Eric." She was dismayed to hear her voice quiver, too.

"I didn't mean to eavesdrop. I picked up the phone thinking it was another call from somebody at ABX."

Jill nodded, finding that easy to believe. "I'm sorry you found out this way."

Only his eyes moved, roaming her features as if searching for someone he'd lost. "Oh? How did you want me to find out?" His downturned mouth looked hurt. So hurt.

Jill ached for him. She couldn't help comparing him to a child whose innocence had been crushed. "I expected you'd remember on your own, someday."

He sat back, his laugh soft and bitter. "Oh, that's funny. What exactly did you expect me to remember, Jill?"

His question confused her. "That we'd decided to separate."

"That *we'd* decided?"

"Yes."

He looked at her hard, his mouth still curled in an expression of bitterness, but uncertainty and self-doubt were beginning to cloud his eyes.

"Oh, Aiden. You didn't think it was all my idea, did you, and I was conspiring behind your back to leave you?" It suddenly occurred to her that nothing in her phone conversation with Eric indicated otherwise.

Aiden looked aside, his mouth tight, the tilt of his head proud. Obviously, he didn't remember. Obviously, he was confused and embarrassed and feeling vulnerable. Jill leaned across the table, reaching for him, wanting to console.

But he pulled back, out of reach, and got to his feet. Everything about the move told her he distrusted her and didn't want her touching him.

He crossed to the family room and crouched before the hearth, elbows to thighs, staring at the cold cinders. Jill's thoughts raced, but among the jumble the only thought that stood out was, This really *was* going to be as bad as she'd anticipated.

Picking up a wrought-iron poker, Aiden idly stirred the extinguished embers. "We're really separating?" From the incredulity of his voice, Jill could only imagine the shock and denial he was suffering.

She moved into the family room, wanting to be closer but knowing he wouldn't let her get too close. Sitting on the sofa, she stared at his broad, tensed shoulders. "That's what we decided."

He put down the poker but continued to stare at the hearth where a fire had burned that afternoon. "I can't remember. Not a damn thing." He ran his hand over the back of his neck. "Maybe you'd better fill me in."

"Aiden, it isn't important."

He turned, glancing at her with eyes so sharp she felt pinned in place. "Fill me in," he ordered in too quiet a voice.

Jill's eyes stung. Although his memory hadn't fully returned, the interlude was definitely over. Like the coolness of a lengthening shadow, she could feel the old Aiden, the real Aiden, advancing on her, coming back.

"I didn't mean our problems were unimportant, Aiden. Just, there's no hurry for you to know about them. We haven't actually split up yet or gone to lawyers or anything."

"Jill," he said impatiently, taking a seat on the raised hearth.

"Okay." She held up her hands to halt further argument. "Where do you want me to start?"

"How about telling me when we made this momentous decision?"

She considered reminding him he had to remember these things on his own, but the warning that came into his eyes told her he wouldn't accept that excuse tonight.

"It was the night before the plane accident. You'd

come home from your trip to Detroit that morning, and we had an argument over your missing Maddy's birthday. One thing led to another," she said, purposely vague, "and by that night it was pretty well decided."

"Our marriage is over because I missed Maddy's birthday?" He looked at her incredulously.

"No. We'd...been having problems for a while."

"What problems?"

When she hesitated, he repeated, "What problems?" in a louder, harsher voice.

"We...just want different things out of life, Aiden. We've grown apart. Let it be, please. My telling you isn't going to do you any good. It'll just get you upset."

"I'm upset already. Tell me." Aiden's eyes flared.

Jill had difficulty speaking. Her throat felt stuffed with cotton. "Your appointment with Dr. Grogan is only two days away. Why don't you wait and have him..."

Aiden curled his left hand into a fist and pounded his thigh. "Why is our marriage on the skids, Jill? I deserve an explanation."

"Okay, okay." She swallowed. Her blood rushed in her ears. "Basically our troubles began when we had Maddy."

Aiden frowned so hard his brows nearly met. Jill didn't want to hurt him any more than he'd already been hurt tonight. She wondered how to say this honestly yet spare him.

"You, um...we hadn't planned on having any children. We got married with the understanding that we'd remain childless."

His scowl deepened. "Why would we not want children?"

"We...had our reasons."

"Such as?"

"Well—" her gaze skittered across the dimly lit room

"—our lives were so busy with work and travel and what-not, we didn't think we'd have the time."

Aiden tilted his head. "I can't imagine you putting work or travel ahead of raising a child. That doesn't sound like you."

She lowered her eyes, hoping to hide the truth from him. He saw it anyway.

"Me? That was *my* reasoning?"

She lifted one shoulder in reluctant admission.

Aiden frowned introspectively. "So what you're saying is *I* was the one who didn't want kids."

Jill had wanted to spare him. She'd tried sharing the blame. But it wasn't working. "I agreed, too. Although I'd originally wanted kids, I adjusted. I accepted your point of view." Jill twisted her interlaced fingers. "But then we had an accident."

"Maddy."

"Yes. My fault, I'm afraid. I messed up with my birth control pills."

"And she changed things between us?"

"Oh, yes."

"How so?"

Jill suddenly realized she'd invested those words "Oh, yes" with too much fervor. Now he wanted details. But details were going to hurt.

She tossed back her long hair with a flick of her head. "They just…changed."

Aiden shot off the hearth and the next moment was looming over her. "How so?" he demanded angrily. "Damn it, Jill, this is like pulling teeth."

She glared back, his anger igniting hers. She'd been trying to spare him, thinking of him as a child who'd been disillusioned. But he wasn't a child. He was Aiden, or would be soon, a grown man who'd coldly decided he had no use for his family because they didn't conform to his agenda. If he wanted her to level with him, so be it, she'd level. "From the moment I told you I was pregnant, you made it clear you wanted nothing to do with her."

"With who? Maddy?" He stepped back, his eyes widening in outraged disbelief.

"Yes. And me, by extension. For the past year you've been gone more than you've been home. You know it, too. You saw your schedule. That was one of the things we argued about the night before the plane accident. You'd only come home that morning and you were flying out again the next day. And, well, I finally reached the point where I felt Maddy and I would be better off on our own."

Aiden lowered himself to a chair. His eyes were narrowed, his lips compressed as if in pain. Remorse suddenly gripped Jill. She shouldn't have been so blunt. She was about to apologize, when he suddenly said, "If you think I'm buying that, you're crazy."

Jill was stunned by his attitude. Her mouth dropped open but nothing came out.

"It's obvious why you're leaving me. I don't know why I bothered to ask for reasons in the first place. Maybe I was just hoping there would be something else."

"What are you talking about?" Jill finally got out.

"It's Eric, just as plain as day. The phone calls, his stopping by, his son always here. And now this, his oh-so-thoughtful advice on divorce lawyers."

"What! Hold it! You're talking nonsense."

"Not as much nonsense as that pack of lies you made up about my not wanting Maddy. How could you say such a thing? How could you think I'd even begin to believe it? I may have lost my memory, but I haven't lost my brain." He shook his head disparagingly. "Are you that desperate to build a case against me?"

True to form, Aiden was too proud to accept blame.

Anger surged through Jill, causing her to speak without weighing her words. "I'm not trying to build a case. What I said was true. Before last week, you treated Maddy as if she was just a piece of furniture. You'd never played with her, never taken her for a walk, never even fed her a bottle. Not one."

"Oh? And this week, clear out of the blue, I'm familiar with feeding her and playing with her and...and loving her?"

Jill bit her lip. She was as lost for an answer to that as he was. He took her silence for guilt and shook his head.

But the condemnation in his eyes soon faded, giving way to quiet sadness. "What I want to know is why. Why did you bother bringing me home?"

He looked so disarmed, her own anger flagged. "You had nowhere else to go."

"So it was pity?"

"No," she asserted, even though she knew pity had played a hand in her decision. "It was just common decency. Respect for what we once had."

"Respect?" he said in scorn. "When you knew I didn't remember we were breaking up? When you let me live in a fool's paradise, speaking and acting as if we were still happily married? That's respect?"

Jill felt her cheeks growing warm. He was angry and humiliated, perhaps justifiably so, and she didn't know how to defend herself or make him feel better.

"Why did you do it, Jill? Was it a control thing? Did you enjoy having me at a disadvantage, helpless even to dress myself? Was it revenge? You wanted to get even for some imagined injustice? Or did you just get a kick out of making a clown out of me?"

Jill knotted with frustration. "Aiden, you've twisted everything around. It was nothing like that."

"Oh, no? Then why did you deliberately mislead me?"

Jill's eyes grew hot and her chest ached. "What did you want me to do? Refuse to bring you home? Make you find an apartment right out of the hospital?"

"That would've been more dignified."

"Dignified? Damn your pride, Aiden!" Her vision shimmered with tears. "You'd lost your memory. You were vulnerable, and the best way for you to get better was to come home. Dr. Grogan said so himself."

"Ah. So you just wanted my memory to come back, and you figured you'd help it along any way you could."

"No!"

"No? Okay, I give up," he mocked. "Why don't *you* explain what this past week's been about? Why don't *you* explain this afternoon?"

Memories of the afternoon assaulted her: lying in Aiden's arms here by the fire, the kisses, the intimacy. Mostly, though, she thought of the promise the afternoon had held for this night, a promise that would never be fulfilled now.

"I have no excuse." Jill hung her head, feeling the weight of her guilt. "Right from the start, it was obvious you'd blanked out most of our marriage, certainly the unpleasant elements. What was left was a man who remembered only the good. You behaved differently, even thought differently." It pained Jill to hear herself speaking in the past tense. "And, quite simply, I liked that new man." A tear slipped down her cheek. "I guess I wanted to pretend he was really you."

"But you believed he wasn't." Aiden's face, she noticed, had become as unreadable as a closed book.

She nodded. "Once your memory fully returns, I know you'll be a different person. Your old habits and attitudes will be back."

"And yet you..."

"Yes. I let things get out of hand. It was a mistake. I know that now, and I'm sorry."

Untouched by her apology, Aiden studied her with cool dispassion, the shadow of his true personality lengthening, advancing on the present.

"I hope you'll understand when I say I don't believe you," he said calmly. "I don't *not* believe you, either. I just prefer to keep my own counsel from now on, or at least until I can discern reality from fantasy on my own and figure out who I can trust. You—" he shook his head, eliminating her from those ranks "—you've proved yourself a little too adept at play-acting."

Jill pulled a tissue from her pocket and blew her nose. "Are you going to move out?" she asked, remembering his readiness to leave before the plane mishap.

His gaze swept over her, cautious and assessing. "Not as fast as you'd like. I know enough about divorce to realize, if I leave, it'll look like desertion, and you'll have more claim to the house and Maddy. No. I'm afraid you've got me around for a while longer. Your impatient friend Eric will just have to wait, and your man-eating lawyer will have to find a different way to sink in her claws."

Jill swiped at her eyes. "I have no idea where to even start on what you just said. So much of it is wrong."

"Is it?" Aiden got to his feet. He began to leave the room, then paused. "Tell me, does anyone else know we're separating?"

Jill shook her head.

"Not even your mother?"

"No."

"Only Eric, then. My, my." He turned and began to walk off again. "Don't bother to come tuck me in tonight, love. The smell of hypocrisy might turn my stomach."

Although it was too early for bed, Aiden retreated to

the guest room, shutting the door firmly behind him. Jill remained curled up in a corner of the couch, immobilized by her grief.

Part of her wanted to run after him. But what would she say? That he was wrong? She'd said that already. He hadn't believed her then and he wouldn't believe her now.

She pressed her fist to her mouth, and her eyes brimmed over again. Damn. She had to get hold of herself. She hated being weak. It accomplished nothing.

Taking a deep breath, she reminded herself that time was on her side. In time, with or without Dr. Grogan's help, Aiden's full memory would return, and when it did, she'd be vindicated. He'd remember his conviction not to have children, remember how assiduously he'd avoided Maddy, and he'd realize she was telling the truth.

But the thought was cold comfort. Vindicated or not, their marriage would still be over. Even if Aiden could somehow change his attitude toward work and family, he wouldn't want to stay married to her. By withholding the truth from him, she'd humiliated him and earned his distrust. To him her actions must seem doubly treacherous because he didn't have his usual grip on the reins of his life. She'd had all the control, and he'd been at her mercy.

The trouble was, Jill understood his viewpoint perfectly. She shouldn't have let him say and do all the wonderful, romantic things he had. How unfair to him. Not only had she accepted his affection, she'd encouraged it, too. If he'd done that to her, she'd be just as humiliated, just as angry.

And just as wrong. For the reality of the situation was, she hadn't set out deliberately to mislead or humiliate him. She'd only wanted him to heal, only wanted to help.

Jill dropped her throbbing head to her hands and softly moaned. No, there was more to it than that. Tonight she'd confessed that she'd let matters "get out of hand" because she liked the person he'd become after the accident. What he didn't know, what she'd lacked the courage to tell him, was that she *loved* that person.

Jill's gaze fell on the rug where Aiden had held her that afternoon. She loved him. She'd warned herself of the danger of letting her heart get involved in his care, but it had happened anyway, warned or not.

Jill looked over her shoulder, down the darkened hall toward the guest room. She could go to Aiden now and tell him what was in her heart. She could explain that love was the reason she'd "misled" him. She could throw herself at him and beg him to forget they'd ever talked about separating. He'd probably listen to her—and he'd probably stay.

But then what? Then what?

Jill laid her cheek on the nubby cushion of the couch, listening to Maddy's soft breathing through the nursery monitor. Who would Aiden be when Maddy woke up tomorrow morning? Who would he be in a week, or a month? Jill wasn't sure, but she had a pretty good idea, and, although she loved Aiden, she wouldn't sacrifice her daughter's well-being for him. Living with a father who didn't want her and continually ignored her would only do Maddy harm in the end.

No, she wouldn't go to Aiden and tell him what was in her heart. He finally understood they'd decided to end their marriage, and regardless of the false reasons he ascribed to the breakup, it was better to let matters lie.

Jill uncurled herself from the sofa, turned off the lights and headed for the stairs. It was early, but suddenly she longed for her bed. She had no desire to experience even one more minute of this particularly heartrending day.

* * *

Jill felt wretched when she dragged herself out of bed the following morning. She hadn't fallen asleep until well after midnight, yet here she was, awake with the birds. She looked wretched, too, she realized, giving the dresser mirror a reluctant glance. She had circles under her eyes and her skin looked sallow.

She sat down on the bed again and considered crawling between the sheets, wishing she could hide there forever. But something inside her, some odd determination, refused to let her do that.

She pushed herself off the bed and into the adjoining bathroom. There, she pinned up her hair and took a quick, bracing shower. She'd been reluctant to get moving, but as she toweled herself dry, she realized she felt much better.

Stepping to the wall-length wardrobe, she slid back one of the mirrored doors and unhooked a pair of jeans and a white blouse. She didn't actually see Aiden's clothing—his things were too far down the closet—but she was aware of them by their faintly spicy scent.

She moved to that end of the closet and slid back the door. His suits and shirts hung in dark, regimental rows. She ran her fingers over a gray wool worsted, then, giving in to temptation, pressed her cheek against the sleeve. She loved Aiden's clothes. Loved the scent of him that lingered in their folds.

Feeling a wave of sentimentality about to swamp her, she abruptly closed the door.

It swamped her anyway. Damn! She couldn't let matters between her and Aiden end this way, muddled by misunderstanding and bitterness. In fact, she didn't want them to end at all.

She stared into the mirror and saw her eyes were wide and frightened. Oh, Lord, what was she thinking?

What you're thinking, she answered herself, *is that Aiden might change.* And why not? If he could be so pleasant and loving with his daughter now, why couldn't he carry that behavior over to the future? It might take work, and he might need help, but help was available in Dr. Grogan. The only thing that was needed was for Aiden to want that change, for him to see it as a valuable direction to take.

He'd never... It isn't in his nature....

Jill gave her doubts a firm brush-off. She wouldn't listen to them today. They might prove true in the end, but right now she needed to keep doors open to the possibility of change, the possibility they could salvage their marriage.

But after last night, what could she do to help the situation?

She gave herself another probing look, and the determination she'd awakened with came surging forward. There were lots of things she could do. For one, she could put away these jeans and pick something more attractive to wear. That cream-colored, tunic-and-tights set Aiden liked so much. And she could put on some makeup and pin up her hair. Well...maybe pinning up her hair was going a bit too far. She much preferred it hanging long and loose. She'd do something different with it, though.

And then, let's see...they'd planned to go to the Cape tomorrow, right after Aiden's appointment with Dr. Grogan. He might not want to go now, but she'd push the idea. Maybe she'd try leaving the baby overnight with Mrs. O'Brien. Getting away, just her and Aiden, was sure to ease the tension between them. It might even rekindle the affection and intimacy they'd recently discovered.

Jill dressed and brushed her hair and applied a light dusting of makeup. Stepping back from the mirror, she gave herself a long, hard glance. She'd do. But she knew she and Aiden had gone past the point where physical appearances swayed anything, especially against problems as serious as theirs.

Last night she'd been stunned that Aiden could believe she and Eric were romantically involved. This morning, however, she understood. If she had overheard Aiden on the phone with some woman, talking about divorce lawyers, she'd be suspicious, too.

She had to address this issue soon, head-on. She and Aiden had enough real problems. They didn't need imaginary ones complicating their lives. More than that, she couldn't abide his believing she'd betrayed him.

She was just tiptoeing out of her room when she heard Maddy stirring. She sighed. She'd hoped to get downstairs and start something special for breakfast before the baby awoke. Oh, well. Aiden really wasn't fussy about breakfast, anyway.

Jill crept down the stairs, Maddy in her arms, thinking Aiden was still asleep. But when she walked into the kitchen, she saw he was already up. He lowered the newspaper long enough to give her an obligatory nod and for her to see he was dressed in a suit.

She stopped in her tracks. "You're going to work?"

"Yes." The chill that emanated from him could've put frost on the windows.

Her heart sank. "But...you can't."

"Why not?" He resumed reading the paper. She was sure he hadn't noticed a speck of her appearance.

"It's too soon."

"Not as far as I'm concerned."

Jill felt she'd been struck. She sat Maddy in her high chair and, swallowing her pain, began warming milk for her cereal.

"Hey, sweetheart." Aiden greeted Maddy with his usual good-morning kiss.

As Jill mixed the cereal, she watched Aiden's interaction with their daughter. At least that hadn't changed—so far. Maybe, just maybe, it would hold.

She pulled a stool up in front of the high chair.

''I'll feed her.'' Aiden rose out of his chair.

Jill was going to protest. His suit would get soiled. But then she thought better of it. The more time he spent with Maddy, the harder it would be for him to leave her later.

''Okay. I'll get her fruit.''

It seemed life was back to normal. Or abnormal. Jill didn't know anymore how to regard the interlude since Aiden's accident. He fed Maddy breakfast. He played peek-a-boo with a dish towel. He made her plush bear dance.

But, of course, life wasn't the same. In spite of Aiden's doting on Maddy, he had nothing but cold disregard for Jill.

And then there was his eagerness to get to work.

''Whoa. Slow down.'' She attempted a smile as she followed him down the hall and into his study.

He didn't look up from the briefcase whose contents he was checking. He only sighed, as if she bored him.

''Aiden, I was wondering—'' She stood by his desk, trying not to wring her hands. ''Our plans to go to the Cape tomorrow? I...''

''Don't worry. I've already canceled the reservations.''

If her heart sank any further, it would soon be in the basement.

''That wasn't what I was thinking. I was hoping we could still go.''

This brought his attention. ''You've got to be joking.''

''No. I mean, we have problems, I'll grant you that. But going away might help.''

He cast her a sardonic look as he snapped the briefcase closed. ''I don't think so.'' He gripped the handle and started for the door. "I'll be taking your car. Okay?"

"Aiden?"

"What." The word was crisp.

"Please stay home. We could go for another walk in the woods, or take a drive somewhere if you prefer. I want us to...get through this."

He looked at her awhile, then blinked and glanced away. "I really have to get to work."

"Damn it! How do you expect us to survive unless you help, too?"

"I'm not helping. But I'm not hurting, either. I'm just being cautious, Jill. I'm waiting till I can see the whole picture. Now if you'll excuse me."

This time Jill let him pass.

CHAPTER EIGHT

HEARING Aiden drive off, Jill seethed with frustration. She grabbed a notepad from his desk and hurled it through the study door. She didn't bother picking it up as she stormed back to the kitchen, where Maddy was beginning to fuss in her playpen.

Aiden had said he was just being cautious, but Jill wasn't dumb. Under that skin of indifference, she could see he was angry. She knew he was still thinking she'd lied to him and their problems were all her fault.

The more she thought about it, the more she began to question his behavior with Maddy, too. She wondered if he'd just been trying to prove Jill was wrong about his not wanting their child. The smug looks he'd occasionally shot her while he'd been feeding Maddy certainly seemed to support that conjecture.

Jill was tired, and his childish attitude acted like tinder on a smoldering fire. As she went about her chores, she found herself slinging pillows, slamming drawers and grumbling audibly.

But her mood didn't last long. As the morning wore on, she realized she was acting just as childishly. She missed Aiden, too. She'd gotten used to having him with her, so much so that by midmorning she felt a vital part of her had been severed. By noontime she'd fully regained her determination to clear matters between them.

She pulled a prime rib from the freezer, thawed it in the microwave and set it in Aiden's favorite marinade. But somehow she didn't think a prime rib dinner was going to do the trick.

What she had to do was address the heart of the matter—Aiden's suspicions of a romance between her and Eric. She thought she knew just how to do that, too. She'd get Eric himself to tell Aiden nothing was going on.

She was supposed to be minding Brady after school today. She'd talk to Eric when he came to pick up his son.

"Aiden went into work today?" Eric seemed surprised when she told him. "I didn't realize he was up to it."

"Yes. He's feeling much better." Jill watched Brady stack a tower of blocks on the living room carpet. Maddy, with satisfying predictability and a minxish giggle, knocked them over.

"Hallelujah!" Eric threw up his hands. "Now you can finally get moving on this separation."

Jill thought his response was a bit ungracious. Most people would first remark on Aiden's returning health.

"Is everything all right, Jill?"

Had she been frowning at him? "Sure. I just have something on my mind."

"Something I can help with?"

"More than you know." With a meaningful look toward Brady, who was old enough to understand adult conversation, she said, "Can we talk out in the hall? I have a favor to ask."

"Name it," Eric said, following her. "You know I'd do anything for you."

Jill paused at the bottom of the stairs, her elbow on the newel post. "I'd like you to talk to Aiden."

"About what?" Eric sat on the steps.

"Well, for some reason, he's acquired a misconception that troubles me, and you, more than anybody, can straighten him out."

"Me?" Eric pulled in his chin. "What's the misconception?"

"That we, you and I, are involved romantically."

Eric's silence puzzled her. She'd expected him to jump in immediately with a response—astonishment, denial, *something.* The color that suffused his face was also puzzling.

"My hope is that you'll talk to Aiden and reassure him nothing of the sort is going on."

Again Eric didn't respond according to her expectations. "Does it really matter what he thinks?" he asked. "You're splitting anyway."

"Eric!" She stood back from the newel post, bristling. "Of course, it matters."

He sat forward, resting his elbows on his knees, and plowed his fingers into his sandy hair. He sighed heavily. "I'm sorry, Jill. I can't."

"You can't?" she repeated, dumbfounded.

"It would be hypocritical."

Slowly his meaning penetrated her confusion. With the dawning came the heat of embarrassment.

"The truth is—" Eric looked up, meeting her eyes levelly "—I do want to be involved with you in that way. I haven't done anything about it yet because I was waiting for the separation to be official. I thought you understood."

The foyer tilted crazily. "I...no, I didn't."

His gaze intensified. "Are you sure?"

"Yes."

He still looked doubtful. "You're not saying that just to ease your guilt, are you? Because if you are, believe me, you don't have to pretend around me, Jill."

She frowned, less sure of herself. *Was* it guilt? *Had* she known their friendship was heading this way?

He reached for her hand and gently pulled her to the step beside him. "Okay, let me put it this way. Would you mind very much if our relationship changed after Aiden left?"

Her first impulse was to say yes, she *would* mind. She couldn't imagine herself involved with anyone except Aiden. Before she could formulate a diplomatic answer, though, he resumed pressing his case.

"We get along so well, Jill." He leaned closer, his expression becoming fervent. "We have so much in common—our hobbies, our children, the same family values. I'm also attracted to you physically. That's something else I thought you knew."

Jill stared at him, speechless, wondering how she could've been so blind. Aiden had seen the truth. Why hadn't she?

"I want to start seeing you, Jill." Eric gripped her by the shoulders. "I want to start taking you out to dinner. Dancing. Exploring all the ways we can be together." He emphasized the word *all* in a way that made Jill feel slightly sick.

She began to tremble. She was sure he could feel it. His hands were still gripping her shoulders. He had to know she was upset. So why didn't he back off? Why was his hold on her softening, turning to an annoying caress?

"So you see, I can't tell Aiden there's nothing between us. I won't do anything to ease matters between you. He doesn't deserve you, and the sooner he's out of your life the better."

Jill had the sickening feeling he was about to kiss her. His head was lowering and tipping to one side. Her pulse rate soared, and on a spurt of adrenaline she pushed herself off the step.

At least she started to.

Unfortunately the front door opened a moment too soon, and there stood Aiden, getting an eyeful.

Jill shook off Eric's hands and finally did get to her feet. If her heart had been racing before, it now beat totally out of control. "Aiden!"

He paused, hand on the still-open door, his gaze moving from her to Eric. Then he gave a huff that might've been a laugh, except he wasn't smiling, and went about his business of hanging his coat and putting his briefcase in his study.

"Eric, you'd better go," she said.

"I'll stay if you think he's going to give you trouble."

"Staying will only make matters worse. Please. You've done quite enough damage already."

Eric got to his feet, hearing the anger in her voice. "You're not mad at me, are you?"

"Yes, as a matter of fact, I am."

He sighed, scrubbing at the back of his head. He didn't argue, though. "Come on, Brady. Get your jacket on. It's time to go home."

After Eric and his son were gone, Jill sat on the step he'd vacated. Her hands, she noticed, were shaking. Aiden crossed the foyer without so much as a sidelong glance, heading for the living room where Maddy was still playing with her blocks.

"Aiden, wait."

Loosening his tie, Aiden turned, giving her a cold, cutting look.

"What you saw, me and Eric…that wasn't what you're thinking."

"Okay, I'll bite," he said with more than a touch of sarcasm. "What was it?"

"I'd asked Eric to talk to you. I wanted him to tell you himself there's nothing going on between us. I figured you'd believe it if it came from him."

"Oh, yes. I can see how eager he was to do that, too."

"That's what I'm trying to tell you, damn it." Her chest felt so strapped with the difficulty of communicating with this stubborn man, it was a wonder she was saying anything at all.

"I owe you an apology, Aiden."

One dark eyebrow arched. That was all the response she got. Obviously Aiden wasn't going to make this easy.

"I was positive there was nothing but friendship between me and Eric. Positive. But he has a different slant on the matter altogether. It seems you were right."

"Big surprise," Aiden muttered.

"Will you try to see my side? Just for one minute? I'm sitting here still shaking. I don't know how it happened, how I didn't see it coming."

"Frankly, I don't, either." His statement was clearly a condemnation.

Maddy toddled out to the foyer. Aiden picked her up and sat with her on the deacon's bench along the opposite wall.

"What did you expect to happen?" He leveled his gaze at Jill. "You and Eric are members of the opposite sex. From what I can see, you've spent inordinate amounts of time together. That's a combination anybody could've predicted would lead to trouble."

Jill dropped her head into her hands and stared at the tips of her shoes. Aiden was right. So why had she let it happen? How had she gotten so deeply involved in a friendship with a man?

She groaned. Maybe she really had known their friendship was on a course toward deeper involvement. Maybe subconsciously she'd wanted it to be headed that way all along.

As soon as the idea crossed her mind, she dismissed it. No, she hadn't wanted a romantic relationship with Eric, even on a subconscious level. She'd shown poor judgment in becoming overly involved with him, but that was her only sin.

And then it came to her. "I was lonely, Aiden. I met

Eric just after Maddy was born. That was a difficult time for me. I don't think you ever understood how difficult."

"Why didn't you come to me?"

"You were gone most of the time, and even when you were home, you didn't care to be around Maddy. As a result, you weren't around me, either."

"That again."

"It's always that." She paused, saddened by the reminder that he still didn't believe that he hadn't wanted a child. He still thought she was lying, laying blame on him to build a case for herself.

"I think unknowingly I went looking for someone to take your place. Not romantically. Never that. Just someone who'd enjoy Maddy with me. Someone who'd *celebrate* her."

Aiden kept his attention focused on Maddy. She was playing with his tie, transferring it from his neck to hers and back again. But Jill saw that his jaw had hardened and knew her words had found their mark.

"I assure you, though," she continued, "nothing inappropriate ever happened, except maybe the friendship itself, and that, I intend to correct immediately."

Her eyes implored Aiden to understand and forgive. His were as cool and unreadable as slate.

"Okay," he finally said.

She waited, but when it became apparent that was the end of his statement, she said, "Okay? That's all you're going to say?"

"What else can I say?"

He could say a lot, she thought, wrestling with resentment, but apparently he didn't want to.

"You still don't believe me, do you?"

Aiden pulled a hand down his face. He looked tired. "A minute ago you accused me of not understanding what a difficult time you went through after Maddy's birth. Well, I don't think you understand how difficult it is to be amnesic. Since waking up in that hospital bed two weeks ago, everything in my life has been fuzz and shadow, in motion, always changing. I've felt completely out to sea. The only sure thing I had was you, Jill. You were my anchor. But yesterday—" his voice sank "—I found out you were just another part of that confusing sea. So you'll just have to excuse me if I'm not exactly chatty right now."

He stood up with the baby and took her into the kitchen. Turning on the lights, he opened a cupboard and picked out a hard teething biscuit.

Jill stood in the doorway watching him as he lowered Maddy into the playpen with her toys. She wanted to cry. Nothing was turning out the way she'd hoped.

"You're wrong, Aiden. I'm here for you. I'll always be here. I'd try to convince you of that, but apparently you've decided not to listen to anything I say. So I'll just wait. Tomorrow you'll be seeing the doctor, and I'm sure..."

"No." He turned from the playpen and gave her a challenging look.

"No? No, what?"

"Forget about me going to the doctor's tomorrow."

"I don't understand."

"You don't have to." He began to walk out of the room, brushing past her.

"Aiden." She caught him by the arm. "You can't just walk away after saying something like that."

"I don't need to see him. I'm coming along fine all on my own. It's as simple as that."

Her eyes narrowed. "What is it?" she persisted.

He lifted his chin defiantly, looking off to one side. "The last thing I need right now is to put myself in the hands of a shrink with Sodium Amytol. I refuse to subject myself to any more humiliation."

"What humiliation? You're not making sense. You

say you don't like being confused, yet you won't go to the very doctor who can help you.''

''Fine. I'm not making sense.'' He pushed on, heading for his study.

Jill stepped in his path. ''Aiden, for heaven's sake, don't turn your back on me. Can't you see how much I care about you?'' She wound her arms around his neck and pressed herself to him.

He remained stiff and unyielding, his arms at his side. ''I don't know what I see, Jill. Yesterday you told me we were breaking up. You said we'd both made the decision. Is that true or isn't it?''

''Yes, but...''

''Well, then.'' He loosened her embrace and advanced one more step, but she was right there with him, blocking his way.

''I'm sorry about this thing with Eric. I really am truly sorry. I don't know how else to say it. I showed poor judgment, and if you suffered any painful suspicions, I apologize. But again I assure you, poor judgment was all that I did wrong.''

''Jill, I don't want to talk about this anymore.''

Jill felt on the verge of tears. He wasn't listening, didn't believe her, and now, on top of everything else, he refused to see the doctor who might help. What if they parted this way, never clearing their misunderstandings?

In her desperation she wrapped her arms around him again. ''Aiden, we've shared too much since you've been home. Think of all that's happened.''

''Jill, please...'' He gripped her arms to set her away from him again. Desperate now, she stood on tiptoe, trying to kiss him. He turned his head and she kissed his cheek. He turned the other way and she kissed his jaw. Angered, she clutched his head in two hands and finally attained her goal.

It was a hard kiss, born in anger and frustration, and one Aiden resisted. His resistance was a sharp reminder that this wasn't doing her a single bit of good. She softened the kiss and then applied every ounce of sensuality she possessed.

By degrees she could feel her husband's body slackening, his resistance weakening. She didn't let up, but rather deepened the kiss, making it long and deep and lush.

He groaned, and before long his resistance had turned to participation. His arms came around her, crushing her to him. Now it was her turn to be assaulted, and she rejoiced in it.

He backed her to the wall, his hard masculine body pressed to hers. She sighed, grateful for the support. His attack on her senses had rendered her knees to water.

He began to explore her mouth with deepened boldness, her body with heated urgency. His hand was under her tunic, rasping her breast and driving her to the edge of crazy...when he abruptly broke away. He was panting hard and his eyes were wild and hot.

"Damn you, Jill!" He stepped back, thrusting his fingers through his hair. "All right, there, are you satisfied?"

She felt slammed. "What?"

"You've proved you still have the power to get to me. Are you happy?"

"I wasn't..." She lifted her hand toward him but he stepped out of reach.

"Stop! Just...stop."

He didn't wait for her to defend herself. She doubted she could anyway. He grabbed up the car keys from the foyer table and, not bothering to put on his coat, stormed out the front door. A moment later he'd driven away.

Jill clutched her arms and doubled over. It didn't help that she understood. It didn't ease the pain or humiliation or sorrow. Aiden had retreated into a shell of distrust and caution, and she really couldn't blame him. She could only blame herself for driving him there.

Jill came awake with a jolt, her body tense, her heart pounding. But then she heard the thunder, diminishing, rolling away in the distance. She sagged into the warm mattress, the tension draining out of her. It was only a storm. Only a spring storm.

She was drifting back to sleep on that consoling thought when a flash of lightning rent the darkness of the bedroom, illuminating the furniture for one stark-white moment. She came awake again, this time with the realization that it was raining and she'd opened one of the windows before turning in.

As the next volley of thunder crashed overhead, she slipped out of bed and crossed to that window. Bringing down the sash, she gazed at her station wagon parked in the driveway below.

Aiden had returned while she'd been giving Maddy her nightly bath. They hadn't spoken, except for her to ask if he'd eaten and for him to answer yes. They hadn't made eye contact, either, but that was fine with her. Their last encounter was still too much with her. She'd made a fool of herself, an embarrassing jackass. Yet, for all her pains, she still hadn't reached him. Now she didn't know what to do. She was out of ideas and, worse, out of hope.

Turning from the window, she switched on a light, retrieved a towel from the bathroom and wiped the rain-slicked, hardwood floor dry. Had she left any other windows open? she wondered. She didn't think so, not at this time of year.

Fully awake now, she had the presence of mind to check on Maddy. She crossed the hall and opened the nursery door a crack. But Maddy was still asleep, her breathing soft and peaceful.

Jill was turning back to her own room when a sudden crash startled her. This crash wasn't thunder, though. She froze in place, listening, eyes wide. It had come from downstairs.

She waited, barely breathing, trying to identify the sound. Was it a picture falling off the wall? A window breaking? Oh, Lord, were they being robbed? But what sort of robber would be out on a night like this? Maybe a limb had broken off the oak tree and cracked a window.

Her curiosity overcame her wariness. She slipped on her robe and tiptoed down the stairs. The rooms below were dark, so Aiden was probably still asleep, though how he could sleep through this storm was beyond her. Not wanting to disturb him, she left the foyer light off and went straight to the living room.

She was just reaching for a lamp when a flash of lightning blasted the room and she saw the silhouette of a man against the window. Her heart leapt to her throat and pushed out a terrified squeak. At the same time, her fingers turned the switch on the lamp.

"Aiden!"

At least she thought she said his name, but she wasn't sure. She was still trying to catch her breath.

She scanned the room and saw a small pedestal table lying on its side, the curios that had been arranged upon it scattered across the floor. Some were broken.

"What are you doing, prowling around in the dark?"

"Go back to bed, Jill." His voice sounded different. She took a step closer just as another clap of thunder cracked over the house.

It was then she noticed the liquor cabinet was open and Aiden was pouring himself a drink. He was half turned away from her, but she was still able to see the decanter shaking in his hand. In fact, he was shaking all over. Somehow he got the glass to his mouth and downed its contents. Then he poured again.

"Aiden, what's the matter?" She rushed forward, all thoughts of their earlier altercation forgotten.

"Nothing. I'm all right." His tone kept her at a distance.

He sipped from the glass, closed his eyes and exhaled raggedly. "Sorry about the table and stuff. I'll clean it up later."

"Don't worry about that. Worry about your feet." He was barefoot, in unsnapped jeans and an unbuttoned blue shirt.

"Did the storm wake you?" she asked.

He nodded and took another swallow.

"Come sit for a while. Just till the storm passes." Jill lowered herself to the sofa and patted the cushion beside her. He looked at it warily. "Keep me company?" she urged.

His movements, walking over and sitting, were slow and tight.

"The storm woke me, too," she said, trying to assume a conversational tone. Lightning ripped across the sky beyond the windows. She stifled a flinch. "Maddy, on the other hand, is sleeping through it like a baby." She glanced at Aiden, but he didn't so much as blink. His eyes were fixed on the space in front of him. He seemed unaware of his surroundings, including her. She sat back, quiet, and waited.

Eventually the alcohol relaxed him. He eased back into the cushions and stretched his long legs toward the coffee table.

"I was dreaming," he said. "A muddled dream. But I got a sense it was about the plane crash." His words were slow and labored. "I felt something awful coming.

I didn't want it to happen. I've had the dream before, a couple of nights now. I usually wake up in a sweat."

"You've been dreaming about the crash?"

"Not in any recognizable form. I don't see the airport or the plane. Nothing specific like that. I just feel the dread, the sense that something terrible is coming." He shivered slightly and took another swig from the tumbler.

It was no wonder he didn't want to see Dr. Grogan, Jill thought. How had he phrased it? Put himself in the hands of a shrink with Sodium Amytol? Sodium Amytol, the "memory drug," a barbiturate that loosened the repressive elements of the brain. Given Aiden's need to be in control, Jill could well understand his reluctance to surrender himself to an Amytol interview, especially when the mental landscape he'd be made to travel under the drug's influence held such terror for him.

Suddenly none of the day's arguments mattered. Jill wanted to hold him, just take him in her arms and tell him it was all right to be afraid. But then he began to speak again and she didn't want to interrupt.

"Tonight the dream changed, though. I think the thunder was beginning to infiltrate my thoughts, I don't know. In any case, there was a lot of noise—deep, rolling, crashing noise. I was someplace..." He raised his broken arm and ran the tips of his fingers over his troubled eyes. "It was a bowling alley. That was it. I was sitting in the lounge of a bowling alley, and I was getting drunk."

He paused, took another swallow of his liqueur, then looked at the glass as if seeing it for the first time.

"Why were you getting drunk?" Jill asked softly, trying not to interrupt him with too intrusive a probe.

"You had just called me. My hotel room. You'd had the baby that afternoon. You'd given birth to Maddy."

Jill sat very still, afraid if she moved even a hairbreadth she'd shatter. "You remember that day?" she whispered.

He didn't answer. Didn't have to. He pushed himself off the sofa, went to the cabinet and laid down the glass. With his back to Jill he stared out the window at the flashing, flickering yard and driving rain.

"You were right. Here I've been putting you through hell, accusing you of having an affair, saying you were lying about me, and you were right." His voice rasped with the grief of defeat. "It was me all along. I didn't want to have kids. I didn't want our daughter. Hell, I wasn't even here when she was born. I was in Atlanta at a business conference. You went through labor and delivery alone."

"I had a birth partner," Jill offered because he seemed so devastated.

"Not me." He laughed bitterly. "It wasn't me." He turned and looked at her with eyes that were red-rimmed and suspiciously bright. "How could I have forgotten something that important for two whole weeks?"

To Jill it was understandable. His attitude was at the heart of the rift in their marriage. It was the issue splitting them apart. In his shoes, she'd want to forget such a heavy onus, too.

She smoothed the folds of her bathrobe. "Do you have any earlier memories of feeling that way? Anything before Maddy's birth? Or is that the only incident that's returned?"

"No, other things've come back. Lots of things. I remember buying my car. You were pregnant. Three, four months maybe." He shook his head and laughed. "A two-seater sports car. Can you imagine?" His face sobered. "What an idiot! I think I was deliberately trying to tell you I planned to live my life the way I wanted, regardless."

"I know," she said, tucking her chin.

"Mostly what I remember, though, is...nothing. Not being here. And that's the saddest part of all. I look back over the past year, and there's so little to recall. Maddy's first year of life is never going to happen again, all that growing she did, all those stages she went through. I watched them from a distance."

"Why?" The question poured out spontaneously because it had plagued Jill so long. "I don't mean, why didn't you want kids. I understand that. Lots of people don't want kids, and they lead perfectly happy, fulfilled lives. My question is, how could you not want your own daughter after she was born?"

He paced, and she could see he was thinking hard. "I have no answer to that," he finally said. "Funny. I sense I should be able to give you an answer, but I'll be damned if the thoughts'll come." He shrugged. "I guess it's just not in my nature to want kids."

He came and sat on the sofa again. "If it's any consolation, I think I wanted to want her. I remember coming home from my trip to Atlanta and seeing her for the first time. She was four days old and just the cutest thing I'd ever seen. But in those four days you and she had already become a team. You'd bonded—against me, I thought. I felt shut out."

"Oh, Aiden. I didn't mean to do that. But maybe you have a point. I was so mad at you." Jill squirmed with guilt, remembering how she'd deliberately shunned him. He'd had three days off, and she'd spent every minute with the baby, ignoring him. "Do you think if I had been more welcoming, there might've been a chance your attitude would've changed?"

"I don't know. Probably not. No. The way I feel seems as ingrained in me as a genetic code."

A knot tightened in Jill's stomach. "The way you *feel?* Does that mean your attitude hasn't changed? You still don't want Maddy?"

He flicked a hooded look her way, then lowered his eyes. Her heart splintered.

"I don't understand it, Jill. I love Maddy. I adore her. But at the same time, this feeling...it hasn't gone away. It's like a shadow that won't stop following me even though I want it to." He pressed his fingers against his eyes. "I still would rather not—" He dropped his hands, exhaling a gust of anguish. "I can't say it." He swore quietly, shaking his head. "This is very confusing. It's like I'm two people locked in the same skin."

Jill felt a trembling deep inside her at the implications of their conversation. "You understand, don't you, that Maddy is an issue I can't compromise?"

"Yes, I know. And I wouldn't want you to." He kept his eyes averted. "But I'm not sure I can change, either. This seems to be who I am, who I'm driven to be."

For several minutes the only sound in the room was the hissing of the rain and the intermittent rumble of thunder, punctuated throughout by the steady ticking of the grandfather clock that had been a wedding present from Jill's folks. Its rhythmic ticks seemed to be asking the question, "What now? What now? What now?"

Jill had no answer. It looked as if Aiden was back. The Aiden who remembered he didn't want his daughter. The Aiden who'd agreed to dissolve their marriage.

The Aiden she did not like.

But was he really? Was the interlude truly over? If so, why was he talking to her like this? The old Aiden would've shut her out and held everything inside.

On the other hand, he'd told her himself that his attitudes were as ingrained as a genetic code. He wasn't going to change. It was dangerous for her to be feeling this softness toward him.

But if his attitudes were that ingrained, where had the behavior of these past two weeks come from? And more importantly, where was it going, now that his memory was back?

A chill ran through Jill right to her core. His memory *wasn't* back. Not completely. Something was obviously still missing—the shadow he'd alluded to that wouldn't stop following him. No, not the shadow. The thing casting the shadow.

Suddenly that "thing" loomed over Jill like a pitched-for-battle enemy she had to fight, a rival whose return would rob her of her husband and Maddy of her father.

"Maybe the best thing for me to do," Aiden said resolutely, breaking into her thoughts, "is move out. I can be packed by tomorrow night."

"No." The vehemence of her response caused him to stare at her. "No, stay a few more days. As you say, you're confused. Give yourself more time."

He rubbed the back of his neck. "I don't know, Jill. I don't exactly like the guy I see emerging. I don't want to impose him on you and the baby too much longer."

"Please, Aiden." A sudden thought struck her. "I want you to keep your appointment with Dr. Grogan tomorrow."

"I told you, I'm doing okay without him."

"Yes, I know. But do me the favor, okay? One last parting kindness. Then—" her heart thumped "—then you can move out."

Aiden sighed roughly. "Okay, I'll go."

"Good." She slumped in relief. "Now, do you think you can get back to sleep?"

"Yeah." He didn't sound too sure, though.

"Would you..." She was about to ask if he wanted to spend the rest of the night upstairs, but then thought better of it.

"Would I what?"

"Like something to eat?"

"No, that drink did the trick, thanks. Go back to bed, Jill. I'm fine."

Reluctantly she got up and headed for the hall. "See you in the morning."

It was still raining when she slipped between the sheets, but the thunder had moved on and was just a rumble in the distance. She turned off the bedside light and sank into the mattress with a pensive sigh.

She honestly didn't know what she'd accomplished by getting Aiden to agree to see the doctor. But at least she'd bought a little more time. She hoped it was enough. Her marriage was depending on it.

CHAPTER NINE

JILL knew Aiden didn't want to see the doctor. From the moment he got out of bed he wore the armored look of a man heading into battle. He ate only one piece of toast for breakfast, and the few words he spoke, even to Maddy, were spare and distracted.

Jill didn't try drawing him out with empty platitudes. She simply moved about as efficiently as possible…and worried.

Quiet guardedness. Pulling away from her. Sinking into himself. Jill knew that behavior well. It was the Aiden she'd come to know after she became pregnant. Was he here to stay? Or was this behavior just an isolated reaction to what he was facing this morning?

Best not to dwell on it. Best just to keep moving.

By 9:00 a.m. Mrs. O'Brien had arrived.

"For lunch there's macaroni and cheese in the fridge," Jill told her. "You know how Maddy loves mac and cheese. And there are canned green beans and pears on the counter. And if…"

"We'll be fine," the woman interrupted, smiling. "Don't you worry about a thing. Hurry along now or you'll miss your appointment."

Jill slipped on her jacket. "I'm not sure how long we'll be. We might…spend a little time in the city shopping." She was improvising, because Mrs. O'Brien still didn't know about Aiden's amnesia. She thought he was simply going for a physical checkup, and Jill was uncertain how much time Dr. Grogan would need.

Aiden came downstairs dressed as if for a funeral, in a dark gray suit, white shirt and black tie.

"Oh, Aiden. You don't have to be so formal." Jill repressed a smile. "Slacks and a sweater would do. *Jeans* would do."

He gazed at her as if from a distance and muttered, "No, I feel more comfortable in this."

He couldn't possibly feel more comfortable, but he might feel more protected, cloaked by an outfit that, to him, represented strength and success and being in command—an outfit that had little to do with his roots and who he was deep inside, where his past lived.

"Okay." Jill backed off. "You look very nice."

They kissed Maddy goodbye, left the house and soon were riding along the wooded rural road that would take them out of Wellington to the highway. As planned, Jill drove.

Still a couple of towns outside the Boston city limits, she turned off the highway and pulled into a train station. She much preferred taking the train to fighting the traffic. Already it was heavy and far too fast for comfort. Within Boston, traffic snarled, slowed by construction, made nerve-racking by impatient motorists. Finding parking was another major headache.

"You know, we don't have to take the train," Aiden said. "I can drive from here."

"Better not chance it. Driving around Wellington with an arm in a cast is one thing. But through the streets of Boston? Uh-uh." She took a ticket from the automated vendor and climbed the ramp into the station's parking garage.

She found a spot, parked and set the brake. As she was gathering up her purse, she noticed Aiden clutching the dash. His hand was white. Her gaze shot to his face. His profile was grim, his eyes fixed straight ahead.

She reached across the seat and laid her hand on his arm. "Ready?"

He broke out of his reverie and nodded, giving her a cursory smile.

The commuter rush was over, and only one other person was ahead of them at the token booth. "I'll take care of this," Jill said, seeing Aiden having difficulty with his wallet.

"Thanks." He stepped back and let her handle the transaction.

When she turned from the booth, Aiden was gone. She had assumed he'd be standing right behind her.

She scanned the sparse crowd milling about the waiting platform beside the tracks. Aiden's height and commanding presence made him easy to find. She pocketed the tokens and walked over to join him.

She'd always found these stations cold, windy places, with their concrete platforms and long tunnel-like roofs. Today, with the temperature a damp fifty-one degrees, she felt downright chilled. Yet when she glanced at her husband, she noticed a sheen of perspiration on his face, a face that didn't look well.

She slipped her hand through his arm and pressed against him. He didn't respond in any way. His eyes remained fixed on the tracks and his thoughts somewhere else.

A train pulled into the station, brakes squealing. Against her side, she felt Aiden tense.

"No, that's not ours," she said. "Want to sit for a while?"

He didn't answer, just kept staring at the train's yawning doors and the people stepping through. A bead of perspiration trickled down his ashen cheek.

Something wasn't right, Jill thought in growing alarm. This wasn't the reaction of a man who was simply reluctant to see a doctor. Something else was going on.

"Aiden?" she asked in an uncertain quaver. "What's the matter?"

He shook his head. "I don't know." She barely heard him, he spoke so low. "I just...would rather not..."

The train moved out of the station and soon disappeared down the tracks. His gaze followed it, his chest rising and falling with breaths that were much too shallow.

Within minutes another train pulled in, this one flashing their destination. Jill squeezed his arm and put on a smile. "We'll get through this. We will. One step at a time," she said, resorting to platitudes, after all.

He grunted, and another bead of moisture rolled down his brow.

The doors slid open and they stepped into the brightly lit interior of the train. Aiden immediately took the first available seat next to the door. He sat on the very edge of the bench, leaning forward, gripping the center pole, exuding all the tension of a sprinter ready to leave the block.

Jill wished she had the power to crawl into his mind, because he certainly wasn't going to tell her what was going on in there. He'd pulled inside himself and closed the hatch tight.

The train began to move, first with a slight jerk, then a smooth glide. She thought she heard Aiden say something, but the rails squealed and she couldn't be sure.

"No."

She definitely heard him then. Her eyes shot to his face in alarm. He looked almost nauseated.

"We have to get off."

"We will, Aiden. In about ten minutes." She hoped she sounded encouraging. "That's all it'll take, and we'll be at the doctor's office."

Aiden closed his eyes and gripped the pole tighter. He continued to lose color. "I...it's happening. I need to get off."

"Ten minutes. We'll be there."

He went whiter, shuddering. "I..." He swallowed convulsively. "I don't need...the doctor."

"I know. We went through this yesterday."

"No. You don't know." For the first time that morning, he looked at her, straight into her eyes. His own were stark and seemed dilated. "We don't need him because I've remembered on my own."

Terrified, Jill stammered, "Remembered what?"

"The last piece of the puzzle. The only part of my life that wasn't in place. Now get me off this damn train, Jill."

Coincidentally, the train slowed and glided to a halt. It wasn't their stop, but Aiden shot from his seat and was out the door immediately, hauling Jill with him.

"Aiden, this isn't our stop!"

"I don't care." Out on the platform, he bent over, hand to his knee, taking in great gulps of air. After a moment, he straightened. He was breathing more evenly, but his eyes still looked haunted, and the color hadn't yet returned to his lips.

"I'm sorry," he said.

"Forget sorry." Jill was still shaking. "Let's go for a walk and talk about this." She took his arm, but he balked.

"I'd rather not."

"Please, Aiden. Whatever it is, you've got to get it out in the open."

He shook his head. "I can't. Not this."

"Why not, for heaven's sake?"

"You...you'll see...me."

"Oh, Aiden." Jill's bottom lip quivered. "I want to see you. All of you. I guarantee, I'll still be here when you're done."

He looked at her long and hard. "I doubt it." But even as he made the dire prediction, he began walking with her.

They left the platform and soon were crossing the street-level parking area. Jill had noticed a grassy verge on the far side, near the highway, and was headed that way.

"It started coming to me as soon as we drove into the last station," Aiden began. "No—before that. I think it's been emerging for a few nights now, in my sleep."

"That feeling you told me about? That something dreadful is about to happen?"

"Yes."

Jill's heart ached for him. Turning into the train station must have triggered the memory of turning into the airport at Wellington. "The plane crash. Oh, Lord. You remembered the plane crash."

But Aiden surprised her. "No. Not the plane crash. The train crash."

She stopped, her feet utterly glued to the pavement. *Train* crash? From the jumble of confused thoughts crowding her mind, there suddenly arose a recollection: Aiden making that same mistake the day he came home from the hospital. She'd considered it a slip of the tongue at the time.

"Train crash? What train crash? When?" she demanded.

They resumed walking at a more contemplative pace.

"I was eight years old at the time, and it was a train between San Francisco and Portland. My parents had gotten divorced a couple of years before. My father moved to the bay area, where he was from originally, and my mother stayed in Portland. A small town west of it, actually. Our house was small and unremarkable, but it was backed by the most amazing forest. Whenever things got too..." He paused, choosing a word. "—unsettled in the house, I used to go for walks in those woods. I think I hoped I'd get lost, but I never did."

Aiden loosened his tie, tugged it off and stuffed it into his pocket.

"Anyway, I split my time between the two places. I lived mostly with my mother and her new husband—she remarried soon after the divorce—but I spent school vacations with my father." He unbuttoned the top two buttons of his shirt and ran his hand around the back of his neck.

"I gather you took the train between the two places."

"Yes."

They arrived at the grassy verge and sat on the curb edging it.

"Did your parents travel with you?"

When he shook his head, Jill swelled with outrage. He'd been so young. Had he been made to travel more than a thousand miles alone? "You traveled all by yourself?"

Aiden rested his forehead on his hand, massaging his scalp with his tensed fingertips. "No. I wasn't alone."

Jill sagged with relief...until he added, "I had my little sister with me."

Jill was struck by the oddest sensation—as if she'd been snatched by a tornado, lifted high into the sky, spun furiously and slammed down to earth again.

"You've never mentioned a sister before. You have a *sister?*"

Aiden's handsome face momentarily crumpled. "Had."

Jill's skin began to crawl with intimations. She suspected she didn't want to hear any more.

"Her name was Becky," he said, regaining his poise. "She was four years younger than me, smart as a whip, and beautiful. Not like me—blond, fair, like my mother. Becky was the kind of child that people—total strangers—stopped to admire."

Jill noticed a change in Aiden's voice, a dreamy,

numb quality about it, as if he'd drifted away from the here and now and was somewhere far and past.

"We, Becky and I, were pretty close, despite the four year age gap. The divorce and all."

He fell into a protracted silence, leaving Jill to fill in the blanks: two young kids pulling together when the world they knew was falling apart.

Then it occurred to her. "Your parents put you on a train in charge of a toddler? When you were a young child yourself?"

"It really wasn't such a big deal. I was used to taking care of Becky. As soon as I got home from school my mother used to hand her over so she could clean the house or run to the market or cook supper before her husband came home."

Jill got a flashing image, a crazy image: Aiden sitting in the kitchen of a tiny fairy-tale house deep in a forest, feeding a baby porridge and making a toy bear dance. She gave her head a shake and blinked until she was back to the present.

But did the present make any more sense? Here she was, a grown woman, sitting on the curb of a parking lot in a town she wasn't even sure she knew, finally getting to know her husband.

"It was the week of February school vacation," Aiden continued. "Third grade for me. I didn't really want to leave to go see my father. I was in a junior basketball league, the first time I had friends in school, and I knew the other guys would be getting together a lot, to play ball and do whatever eight-year-old boys do during school vacation. But my mother liked her free time." His lips gave a twist that spoke volumes. "So off we went, Becky and I."

He hunched forward, elbows on his knees, his hands bracing his forehead. Jill thought he shivered.

"I know it's hard, Aiden." She ran her hand across

his back, encouraging him, she hoped. "But continue if you can."

He nodded. "It was snowing. A freak storm. The trip was slower than usual, and Becky was more rambunctious than usual. The combination wasn't good, especially since I was already mad about having to leave my friends."

Aiden got up quite suddenly and paced back and forth, his polished black shoes crunching the sandy debris on the edge of the asphalt lot.

Jill looked up, wondering if she should suggest he quit for now. She had no intention of letting him bury the episode indefinitely, but she could wait until he felt stronger.

He seemed to read her thoughts. "No, I've started. I might as well finish." He sat on the sun-warmed curb again, determination in the set of his jaw.

"Becky kept getting up out of her seat and wandering the train car, talking to people, wandering into the next car, talking to people there. I kept telling her to sit down, but she wouldn't listen, and finally I just gave up. I knew she couldn't go far. The next car was it. The door at the other end was locked. And it wasn't like anybody could kidnap her or anything. So fine, I said. Go wander, get out of my hair. Now I can read my comic books in peace."

During the eerie pause that ensued, Aiden's skin went as gray as granite. "Then what?" Jill urged quietly.

"I don't know exactly how it happened. Human error. The snow. A failed signal. All I remember is the impact and being thrown around. There were screams and people getting up and falling on me...and a sound I'll never forget. Metal crunching. It seemed to go on forever." He shut his eyes tight. His cheek muscles quivered. Jill ached as if his pain was her own.

After a moment his eyelids lifted and he said in an

empty voice, "I couldn't find Becky. I tried to get out of my seat, but people were in the aisle, pushing and clawing. I called for her, and called."

Jill felt a tear fall on her knee and realized in surprise that it was her own.

"It was no use, though." Aiden's broad shoulders slumped. "She'd been in the other car, the car that took the brunt of the hit from the other train." He covered his eyes with his hand. Jill didn't know what to do, but then he lifted his head and in a more ordinary voice asked, "Can we skip the next part?"

Jill rubbed his back and felt strong muscles trembling under her hand. "Sure, Aiden. Of course." She laid her cheek on his shoulder.

Several heartbeats later he continued. "My mother took it hard. She may have had her faults, but she loved Becky. Becky was her favorite. She collapsed at the funeral."

Jill gasped. "Oh, she didn't... That isn't when she...?"

Aiden looked at her, confused. Suddenly his brow cleared. "Oh, no. My mother...my mother isn't dead. She's very much alive and living in Oregon, still."

Jill felt another one of those tornadoes picking her up and spinning her around.

"I told people she was dead because to me—" Aiden's jaw hardened "—she was. You see, she blamed me for Becky's death and she never forgave me. She sent me to live with my father, and I haven't seen her since."

Jill sat speechless. She couldn't imagine a mother who could do such a thing to her child, especially knowing how close he was to his sister, how responsible he must've felt, being the big brother.

"Aiden, it wasn't your fault. You couldn't have

stopped the snow or the faulty signal or whatever caused the accident."

"That's what I tell myself when the guilt gets too bad, but sometimes I wonder. Why couldn't I have had a little more patience with Becky? I could've read to her or played a game, something to keep her in her seat."

"Aiden, listen to me." Jill turned and, grabbing his shoulders, shook him as roughly as she could budge a one-hundred-ninety-pound man. "It was not your fault. Kids get squirmy. They move around. And accidents, by their very definition, happen when we least expect them."

He only sighed and squinted off into the distance.

"I have an odd question, Aiden. Was this train crash something you've repressed for years? Did it just come back now?"

"No. This is the first time I've been amnesic—if that's what you're asking." He smiled faintly—a wry, self-deprecating smile. "I've been aware of the crash since it happened."

Her heart broke for him. "What a burden. You should've told me."

"I couldn't."

"Why not? Did you think I'd blame you, too? Think less of you?"

"Yes."

"You are crazy." She wrapped her arms around him and rocked him with all the affection within her.

He rested his chin on the top of her head and stroked her hair. "When we got married, I thought I'd finally put all that behind me. Everything was turning out as I'd hoped. I'd made a new life for myself far away from my roots. I was rising at ABX. I was happy." He pulled back and looked at her, his eyes avid. "Very happy."

Even as she savored the compliment, Jill was seized by an unexpected chill, as if a dark shadow had overtaken her. Staring into Aiden's eyes, she finally understood. "And then I got pregnant," she said.

He nodded. "And all I could think was, I can't do this again. I can't take responsibility for another child. I was certain I'd fail it, too, somehow. I'd be a bad father, bring harm to it in some way."

"That was a totally irrational fear, you know."

"No, I didn't know that," he said impatiently and with a touch of vehemence.

Jill stared at him numbly. In some corner of his mind he'd believed his mother.

"As far as I could see, the best thing I could do for the child was keep my distance."

Jill sighed. "I wish you'd told me."

"And what would that have accomplished?"

"I would've understood."

"Understood what? How irresponsible I really am?"

She shot him a glare. "I would've understood why you were so distrustful and afraid to love. You'd been hurt by the two people you loved most in the world. Becky, by her dying, and your mother, by her rejecting you."

"Jill, I'm in no mood for amateur psychology."

She tried not to feel insulted. "Are you in the mood for the professional sort?"

He shook his head, looking exhausted suddenly. "I just want to go home. By cab, if you don't mind."

Reluctantly, Jill got to her feet and they began to walk toward the terminal where they could call for a taxi.

Aiden was quiet. Too quiet. Jill began to burn with a new worry. She paused, frowning at the asphalt.

Two steps ahead of her Aiden stopped and turned. "What's the matter?"

She looked up, tensing, feeling the enormity of the moment. "After we get home, are we going to be okay?"

Aiden didn't answer verbally but Jill saw what he was thinking in the evasiveness of his eyes. Her blood ran cold.

"Aiden, no." She seemed to be inhaling her words. "Don't you dare cut out on me. Not now."

He thrust his hand through his hair. "Just because I have that stuff in my past, Jill, that's no reason to excuse the way I acted toward you and Maddy."

"Well, of course, it is."

He shook his head adamantly. "That's rationalization. A bucket of excuses. Actions are what's important."

Jill pressed a hand to her trembling midsection. Last night she'd imagined the "thing" lurking in Aiden's past as her enemy, a rival threatening to steal him away. Right now, she felt that enemy was winning.

"Aiden, if I can forgive you, I think you should, too."

He glanced at her just long enough for her to see he wasn't convinced.

"Besides," she said quickly, "I wasn't completely innocent of faults, either. I bailed out on you much too soon. I should've been more understanding, but instead I locked you out and turned to a perfect stranger."

"You had reason."

"No. What I had was inappropriate expectations. I kept comparing our marriage with my parents', you to my father. I should've known better. Every marriage is different." She gave him an imploring look. "I'll forgive you if you'll forgive me. That's what love is all about, I think." She blinked away the blur of fresh tears. "That, and moving on."

"Well, see, that's the thing." Aiden resumed a shuffling pace. "I'm not sure I can move on. I'm still that same person, Jill. Just because I told you about my mother and Becky, you think I'm going to be different?"

"Yes, because you are different. You're sensitive and strong and conscientious."

"Oh, yeah." His lips curled sardonically. "So strong and conscientious I bugged out for two whole weeks after a minor plane accident. Is that the sort of man you want for a father to Maddy?"

"Exactly the sort."

He shot her a skeptical sidelong glance.

"You talk about actions... Don't you know what you did on that plane?"

"Yeah. I had a flashback to Becky's death, couldn't take it and jumped down a mental rabbit hole."

"Not entirely. You helped other passengers get off the plane first. I kept watching for you, but you were one of the last people off. You were helping the medics and flight attendants with others. Even with your broken arm. That's the sort of man you are, Aiden."

His doubtful eyes met hers as they paused yet again. "Where'd you hear that?" A car honked, and barely aware of it, they stepped out of the way, onto the sidewalk.

"From Dr. Grogan. He heard from the airline. I think they're planning to send you a commendation."

Aiden tilted his head. "Well, I'll be damned!"

"If that isn't enough, think about how you've acted with Maddy these two weeks." Jill gripped his arms and gave them an emphatic squeeze. "*That*'s you, too, Aiden. All that love, all that caring. It's inside you, just waiting to get out. It's been there all along."

He looked at her—finally listening, she thought.

"The question now is, are you going to let your past continue to overshadow it? Are you going to let it control your life?"

Aiden's dark eyebrows lifted into an awakening arch, and she knew she'd found her weapon in the word *control*.

Jill didn't let up, though. "Are you going to let the past ruin our marriage? Rob Maddy of a father she loves?'' The more she realized what was at stake, the more impassioned she became. She felt she was fighting a life-or-death battle.

''Aiden, it's all there. You just have to bring that person out of the shadows, and keep him out, permanently. Don't walk away from him. He's your life with me and Maddy. He's your happiness. He's...*you.*''

''Jill, don't cry.''

''Don't leave me then,'' she sobbed. ''I love you.''

Tears in his own eyes, Aiden reached for her and crushed her to him. ''Oh, God. I love you, too. I always have. You're my life, Jill. I love you so much I ache with it.''

''Well, then.'' She laughed through her tears. ''Well, then...''

He kissed her, a kiss full of affection and gratitude and hope.

''It won't be easy.'' Aiden looked at her levelly. ''I don't even know if it'll work. But I'll give it a try.''

''Of course it'll work.'' Jill held him to her, laughing.

''How can you be so sure?''

''Because it's working already.''

Aiden's blue eyes glittered down on her. ''When did you get to be so wise?''

Jill didn't have the chance to answer, though, because he dipped his head and kissed her again. Just beyond, a train glided into the station, its brakes squealing along the tracks. When it pulled out a few minutes later, she was still being kissed.

CHAPTER TEN

One and a half years later

BY NOONTIME on that clear September day, thirty-five guests had arrived, most bearing a favorite dish to add to the potluck table Jill had set up in the sunroom. In spite of the surfeit of food, Aiden was also preparing to fire up the grill.

"Do any of your friends realize it's your anniversary?" Jill's mother asked from the cooking island in the kitchen where she was garnishing a potato salad with sprigs of parsley.

"A few do, but we asked them not to say anything." At the sink Jill slipped the aluminum basket into the thirty-cup urn and reached for the canister of coffee. "Most think we're simply having an end-of-summer cookout. And we are. The fact that Aiden and I were married five years ago today is incidental."

The kitchen door opened and Jill's father strolled in, wearing an oversize barbecue apron. "Aiden wants to know if there's any more lighter fluid."

"In the garage, Dad. Back wall. Top shelf."

On his way past her, Charles gave his daughter a glancing kiss on the cheek. She smiled, her heart filling with contentment. Her parents had flown east a couple of days ago with a double-edged mission. They were here to visit with their daughter and son-in-law, of course, a visit Jill was enjoying immensely, but primarily they'd come to stay with Maddy while Jill and Aiden were off on a week-long cruise to the Caribbean, a second honeymoon of sorts.

Jill carried the coffee urn out to the sunroom and placed it on the beverage table.

"Is there anything else I can help with?" her mother asked, following with the potato salad.

Jill scanned the room and shook her head. "Thanks, but everything seems under control. Why don't you find yourself a chaise and relax for a while?"

"Sounds like a great idea," Mildred agreed and wandered outside. But before she got a chance to sit, Maddy found her and dragged her off toward the swing set where several other children were playing.

Jill watched them walk off hand-in-hand and smiled. At two and a half, Maddy was not only a physically beautiful child, she'd developed a delightfully engaging personality, as well, with only occasional bouts of stubbornness to remind the world that she was in the terrible twos.

Jill's gaze moved from her daughter and mother over the rest of the yard. Around the vibrantly green lawn, just recovered from the heat of the summer, annuals were at their zenith—impatiens and marigolds, cosmos and zinnias—each lending an explosion of color to the subtler shades of the fall-blooming perennials. Jill was pleased by her gardening efforts this year, but even more pleased at seeing so many of her and Aiden's friends enjoying them.

Among those friends was Eric Lindstrom. When Jill spotted Eric, she emitted an unsuppressible chuckle. He appeared to be conducting a nature tour, as he tramped through her woodland gardens, pointing out this plant and that to a trailing group of not-so-interested listeners.

Eric, as it turned out, wasn't such a bad sort after all. After the misunderstanding involving his relationship with Jill, guilt had worn him down. A week after the unfortunate incident, he'd returned to apologize, but by then Aiden hadn't needed to hear his side of the story to know there was nothing illicit going on. Since then Eric and Aiden had remained, if not fast friends, at least cordial neighbors.

Just then Stan Grogan arrived, coming around the side of the house, looking fit and tanned in khaki shorts and a yellow knit shirt, a tennis racquet tucked under one arm. He'd been *Doctor* Grogan until the previous winter, when he'd officially given Aiden a clean and complete bill of health, and then he'd become Stan to them, a frequent guest at their dinner table and a close personal friend.

Not only had he helped Aiden lay all his old ghosts to rest, among them his guilt over his sister's death, Stan had even suggested that Aiden travel to Oregon and make amends with his mother, which he did, and which helpled him come to terms with the past.

Stan had also guided Aiden to a far more balanced way of life, for which Jill would be forever grateful. Although Aiden was still very much the rising executive at ABX, he'd cut back on his hours and business trips and was now spending a lot more time with his family.

Jill watched Aiden greet Stan now, introduce him to her father, and put the two men to work lighting the grill. Then he turned and started for the house.

He was wearing comfortable jeans and a blue oxford shirt, its long sleeves rolled to expose strong, tanned forearms. His handsome face creased into a smile as soon as he spotted Jill, standing just inside the sunroom, watching him.

"Hey, Jill, could you help me with something?" he asked, stepping into the house.

"Sure. What's up?"

But Aiden didn't explain immediately because several other people were in the room, hovering over the food table. He took her arm, led her down the hall and up the stairs to their bedroom, where their luggage waited, packed for their cruise and ready to be carried to the car in the morning.

"I don't really need your help with anything," he confessed, shutting the door. Suddenly he was all seriousness. "I have to ask you something."

"What is it?" Jill had begun to tense on the stairs. Now she was downright worried.

Still holding her arm, Aiden guided her to the bed and motioned for her to sit. She noticed he was breathing rather more rapidly than normal.

"I was going to surprise you, Jill," he said, scowling as he sat beside her, "but the more I thought about it, the riskier it seemed. My surprise could backfire and embarrass us all—you, me and everybody here."

"Aiden, what?"

He took in a deep breath and let it out in a gust. "You're aware that Bill and Muriel Hunter are here, right?"

"Of course." That was the last thing she'd expected to hear. "I invited them myself."

"Well, Bill's here in a double capacity. As a guest, of course—" Aiden blinked rapidly "—but also as our minister." When Jill's puzzlement deepened, he explained, "You see, I arranged for him to conduct a small ceremony today."

"Ceremony?" Her brow creased.

"Mmm." He cast an uncertain glance her way. "A renewal of our wedding vows."

Jill's breath hitched.

"I was going to ask you in front of everybody out there, but then I got to thinking. What if you didn't want to renew your vows? What if you said no, or worse, went through it against your will just to spare me the embarrassment?"

Jill stared at her husband, wide-eyed and still, trying to take in everything he was saying.

"So," he continued, "I decided to ask you first." He took her two hands in his and held them tight. He looked frightened to death. "Jill, if you had the chance to do it all over again, would you marry me?"

Jill's lips parted in mute astonishment. Her once-guarded, undemonstrative husband had arranged a second wedding ceremony?

"If you think you'd rather not..." Aiden backpedaled, misinterpreting her silence. "I understand. I should've consulted with you first. I don't know what ever possessed me to think you'd enjoy being surprised."

"No, Aiden, I do like the idea," she said, finally finding her voice.

His head snapped up. "You do?"

"Yes, I love it. And to be proposed to again... It's the most romantic thing that's ever happened to me, even more romantic than the first time. Of course, I'll marry you again." She laughed. "Did you really think I wouldn't?"

He looked a little sheepish. "Well, I wasn't sure. These first five years haven't all been a bed of roses."

Jill's grin widened as she wrapped her arms around his neck. "I'm glad you don't take me for granted, but, oh, Aiden, I love you so much you should've..."

Before she could say another word he kissed her, murmuring that he loved her, too, and by the time he lifted his head again she'd forgotten what she'd intended to say.

"Come on, then." Smiling, Aiden got to his feet. "Let's go surprise our friends." He reached for her hand and she started to get up.

"Wait." Jill pulled her hand from his and sat down again. "I have something to ask you, too, and maybe I should ask before we go through with this ceremony."

A look of anxiety returned to Aiden's face. "What is it, Jill?"

She kept her eyes fixed on his expression. "How would you feel if I were to tell you we—" she gulped "—were going to have another baby?" Her heart pounded, and with good reason, she thought. Aiden's aversion to having children had run deep, and despite the success he'd had in overcoming his past, despite even his agreement several weeks ago to start trying to conceive, she still feared that in some dark recess of his personality that aversion might still be alive.

Holding her breath, she watched his eyes. If she'd had any lingering doubts, Aiden's expression dispelled them instantly. His face lit up like the sun breaking through clouds.

"Oh, my God, Jill!" He laughed in unadulterated joy. "Are we really?" When she nodded he swept her into his arms and twirled her 'round and 'round, nearly toppling over their suitcases. He was still laughing when he finally set her down.

"How long've you known? When are we due?" he asked on one excited breath.

Unexpectedly Jill's eyes grew hot with tears. His response was everything she'd ever dreamed, and more. "I took a home pregnancy test a couple of days ago, another one this morning. Both came up positive. I figure it's going to be another spring baby. Maybe May this time."

"And how are you feeling?" He ran his hands along her arms.

"Fine. A bit tired, but at least there's no sign of morning sickness."

"Are you sure? We can cancel this cruise if..."

"No! Really, I'm fine."

Aiden finally seemed convinced. "Great," he murmured, nodding. Then he looked toward the door. "Do you want to make an announcement?"

From the gleam in his eye, Jill sensed he was eager

to tell the world, which pleased her immensely, but her own instincts shied away from sharing the news just yet. "Let's wait another month or so, okay? It's still pretty early in the pregnancy."

He nodded, understanding. "Sure. Well..." He grinned and scrubbed at his dark hair, looking proud and endearingly boyish.

Laughing softly, she took him by the hand. "Come on, Dad. We'd better get downstairs before people think we've deserted our own party."

Outside, from the vantage point of the deck, Aiden called everyone to gather 'round. The children came running from the swings, and the nature tour straggled out of the woods.

Once all their curious guests had closed in, Aiden said, "Jill and I have a confession to make. We didn't invite you people here just so you'd bring us all this great food. Today also happens to be our fifth anniversary."

A chorus of surprise rose from their friends. "Why didn't you tell us?" several people asked.

Shrugging, Jill answered, "We wanted to keep it low-key, just be with our friends here at home. Lots of good food, maybe a badminton game or two. There seemed no better way to celebrate."

Maddy clambered up the deck stairs, her golden hair, tied in two bouncy pigtails, gleaming in the sun. Aiden picked her up, propped her on one arm and continued, "Before we get on with the day, though, we do have one favor to ask."

Jill felt a giddy tremor ripple through her. Her fingers curled around Aiden's arm as he explained, "Jill and I have decided to renew our marriage vows today, and we'd like you to share in the event."

That announcement caused a loud response, half surprised gasp, half romantic sigh, all unequivocally thrilled.

"I see Reverend Hunter already has his book open, so if you'll follow us..." Aiden, still carrying Maddy, led Jill down the steps and across the lawn toward a rose arbor heavy with summer's last flush of bloom.

Mildred, her chin slightly tremulous, sidled up to Jill and whispered, "What a man! When you picked him, you really knew what you were doing." Then, turning to Aiden, she offered to take Maddy off his hands during the ceremony.

But Aiden answered that she was no trouble. "Maddy's as much a part of this ceremony as we are," he said, a sentiment that put a tightness in Jill's throat that wouldn't release.

Her parents took a favored spot up front near the arbor while the rest of the delighted gathering formed a loose semicircle behind them, and the ceremony began.

"Dearly beloved, we are gathered here..."

Jill tried to focus in on the minister's voice, but she felt as if she'd stepped into a dream. His words floated around and over her like iridescent bubbles blown from a child's wand. She felt fairly light herself, floating in the mellow September sunshine, and the only thing keeping her grounded was Aiden's hand at her waist.

Turning, she looked up at Aiden and found he was gazing back at her, his eyes soft and burning with love. She smiled, returning that love, while the minister intoned, "Do you, Jill Kruger Morse, reaffirm your commitment to this man, Aiden Allen Morse..."

The ceremony proceeded, simple and quick. I-do's got exchanged, vows reaffirmed and the minister's benediction bestowed, all within the span of five minutes. But if time could have depth as well as length, Jill thought, then surely those brief few minutes were as deep as any sea, as high as any sky.

"...For better or for worse, richer or poorer..." Simple, familiar words, but when Jill spoke them this second time around, five years' worth of married life resonated through them, enriching them. When Aiden said, "In sickness and in health," she knew that he, too, was looking back as well as forward and experiencing the resonance and texture of the moment.

And when they repeated, "Till death do us part," they both knew they meant it in a way that had been beyond them the first time through. Aiden heard in Jill's conviction a steely strength that came from surviving the forge of adversity. Jill heard in Aiden's voice a commitment totally free of reservation, purified in that same hard fire of adversity.

With the ceremony over, Aiden kissed Jill tenderly but all too briefly because Maddy was still in his arms. He was about to put her down when Jill's father called, "Hold it. Don't move. My camera's in the house."

"Oh, I want to get a picture, too," someone else said, dashing for her purse.

And so Jill and Aiden stayed where they were, standing under the rose arbor, Maddy in the circle of their arms, while friends extended congratulations and cameras clicked and whirred, capturing the moment for all time.

"You'll send us copies, I hope," Jill called when the picture-taking had waned.

And Aiden said, "Thanks, everybody," while finally setting his daughter on her feet. "You've helped make this day really special for us. Now—" he rubbed his hands together "—let's get to the food."

Laughing, the crowd broke ranks and began to make its way to the house, with Jill and Aiden strolling behind them.

Jill had so much she wanted to say to her husband, her heart was nearly bursting with it. But she knew that this was neither the time nor the place. Telling Aiden how deeply she loved him and how much this ceremony meant to her would have to wait for a quieter, more private moment.

For now she'd have to be content with simply saying, "Thank you, Aiden."

He fit his hand around her waist and pulled her closer to his side, understanding tacitly what she meant. "I'd say we just created a jewel of a memory there. What do you think?"

Jill nodded, agreeing. "We're going to have so many wonderful things to remember about this anniversary—not just that ceremony, but this get-together and our cruise..."

"And your little announcement," Aiden added.

His reminder sent happiness streaming through her. "Yes. So many good things. This day has been...our *life* has been..." She paused, at a loss for a way to describe what she meant.

"Unforgettable?" Aiden supplied.

Sharing a meaningful smile with him, she agreed. "Yes. Unforgettable."

Aiden pressed a kiss to her forehead. "Do you know what the best part is, love?"

"What?"

"We've only just begun."

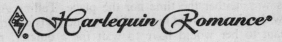

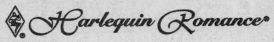